LEGEND OF THE SLEEPING DRAGON

Book One

By Lasalle Johnson

Cover designed by Kay M. McDaniel

First Printing: Dec 2020
Gary, IN
Identifiers: Library of Congress Control Number: 2020923049

ISBN 978-1-7353920-1-1

CONTENTS

THE BEGINNING

This story began in Europe during the early 14th century with a small society of people who dwelled deep inside the woods in a town called Inglewood. The people of Inglewood were a peaceful group of people who didn't believe in the luxuries nor the ways of the city people. They followed in the ways of their ancestors, who lived and tilled off the land. Nathen and his wife Betty were both raised in Inglewood and together they were raising their two children there with the hope that one day their children would do the same. Nathen enjoyed working with his hands. He spent most of his time working, building, and repairing things throughout the town just as his Father and Grandfather once did. All though they both had been skilled carpenters, perhaps the best of their time, he knew without a doubt that he was not only the best of his time but also the best of the three. The past few years had been good to Nathen. He had everything a man could ask for. A loving wife who adored and treated him like a King, an eight year old son named Chase who watched him and also wanted to be a carpenter just like him and a six year old daughter named Zora who would flood him with kisses every time he got home from work. They owned a large piece of land with a big house. They also had goats, cows, ox and chicken. The couple had all they needed. Things were great and the future looked bright. Nathen was out gathering wood on an early spring morning when he heard the sound of footsteps quickly coming in his direction. Holding an axe firmly in his hand to scan the area to see who or what was approaching him. Over the years he had encountered many dangerous animals and situations and like all woodsmen, he mastered the skill of awareness and how to hold his own with an axe. He stood statue still and waited for the creature to reveal itself but instead he spotted Albert, a store man from his village running in his direction. "Run! Run!" The man yelled in a panic as he waved his hands from side to side. His shirt drenched in blood and his pants were ripped as if he had snagged them on a tree.

Not sure what to make of the situation, Nathen asked, "What's going on?"

"Inglewood is under attack!" the fat man yelled. He ran past Nathen with no intention of stopping.

"Run and save yourself." he screamed, and he kept running.

Nathen's heart dropped into his stomach. He could not believe what he had just heard. The witch hunts had started again. He had hoped his children would never have to experience the nightmare that haunted his mind every time he closed his eyes. Nathen was only seven when the priests attacked his village with an army of soldiers killing all who opposed their religion or the demand to convert. Nathen charged through the woods fast jumping over logs and crashing through switches and tree branches. His primary thought was getting to his family although he had no idea how he would save them. He just hoped they had made it to the town hall to get in the secret safe house hidden in the building. Nathen arrived at the village too late. Bodies laid everywhere. The blood of his fellow townspeople made the dirt red and muddy. He rushed to the town hall, but found the building burnt down. He starred at the rubble in disbelief. The meeting hall that once saved his generation was now a collapsed pile of burnt wood, black brick, and ash. No other buildings were burned down. Somehow, the soldiers knew about the secret room and torched the building because of it. Not thinking, Nathen attempted to search the rubble for survivors. He reached in to grab a plank of wood but snatched his hands back. The debris was too hot. Deep down, he knew there were no survivors. Everyone inside would have been burned alive for sure. Suddenly the thought of his family being captured seemed better than the thought of them being burned alive. It was the hope for a lesser evil. Either way he knew he would never see them again. Those whom were captured by the Priests army were taken back to Rome and most likely sold into slavery. Sorrow overpowered him. All that he loved was taken away in one horrible sweep. Extreme pain surged throughout his body. He no longer had a reason to live. A man is supposed to protect his family, he told himself. He dropped to his knees in an ocean of tears and pounded his fists hard against the ground letting out a loud cry. He beat the ground until he had no strength and then he passed out. Nathen awoke the next morning, his fists swollen and crusted with blood. Yesterday's events were right there in his head as if it waited for him to awake.

"Why did this happen?" He asked the Gods. "What did I do to deserve this?" he yelled.

He looked across to the children's playground. A large pine tree held a swing and a big wooden crate was beside the tree. Tears started to fall. The swing reminded him of his own children. He no longer had the will to live so he decided to take his life. Then he wrapped the rope firmly around a branch on the tree. He placed the crate under it. He stood on the crate. He put his head through the noose. “Family, I’ll be with you soon!” he said, and then he jumped. The rope squeezed around his neck tightly cutting through his skin. The pain was unbearable. He clawed at the rope to set himself free, but his attempts were in vain. Reality sunk in. There was no stopping the process. His body shook uncontrollably, and he felt his veins were about to explode. In agony, he let out a silent cry. Suddenly, the ground began to shake and time itself began to slow down. Suddenly, it stopped, and his pain immediately disappeared. Nathan tried to move but he was paralyzed. He realized he was frozen in time.

“What is this?” he wondered.

“A place not known to men.” a voice replied.

Lava sprang from the earth as it quaked. It began consuming everything in its path. Within seconds, he was enclosed in a box of hot lava coming up from the ground. Suddenly he was able to see a silhouette. Its features were that of a human but mixed with various animals. He had long black bat wings that twitched on his back. His upper body was dark red and muscular although he appeared to have a normal human upper body. His legs were covered in brown fur with a long tail that reminded Nathen of a ram or goat except he walked on two hooves.

“Who are you?” Nathen asked the creature frightened of what was about to befall him.

"I am known by many names, but you can call me the devil."

"Are you here to collect my soul? Am I dead?"

"That will depend entirely on you. I've come to propose a deal. One that we both get what we want. My proposal is simple. I want you to write my book."

"I don't understand! Why can't you write your book?"

"Because, I am of the spirit world, in order for my book to exist on your plane of existence, it has to be written by a physical being. It will be easy. I'll tell you what to write and you just write it. In return, I'll make you stronger and more powerful than any human being on this earth. Then, you can take your revenge on those who killed your family."

"So, my family is dead?"

"Perhaps, but there is only one way to find out."

Nathen agreed to the devil's terms. Instantly, he was back in the physical world standing on solid ground. The tree and the noose were only a few feet behind him. A familiar looking man stood in front of him.

"This is me in my human form." the devil said. He walked up to Nathen and handed him a small vile with a red liquid inside.
"Drink this!" he ordered.

Without any hesitation, Nathen drank the whole bottle. He handed the bottle back to the devil.

"Now what?" Nathen asked.

"So eager!" the devil laughed. "Give it a minute."

At that moment, Nathen dropped to the ground and his body went into a seizure. Unable to scream, tears escaped his eyes. He looked up at the devil as if he expected him to help, but he just stood over him with that silly smile on his face.

"By now you're feeling your bones break." the devil explained, "But trust me, it will be worth your suffering."

The devil watched Nathen as he went through his agonizing transformation. Then right when Nathen reached the pain level between being conscious and passing out, he looked Nathen in his eyes.

"I've given you some of my blood. With it, you've gained some of my powers. Just remember our deal." he said, and then he disappeared.

Nathen came too with the moon glaring in his face and the stars shinning bright. For some reason the moon seemed closer to him. So close, he felt he could touch it. His sense of hearing improved. He could hear the bats in the far-off cave. Their wings were flapping as if they were next to him. Nathen smiled at the birth of his new powers. He felt energized, stronger and faster. All his senses were inhuman and beyond belief. He knew he could take on the whole Roman army if need be. Now was the time to take his revenge. He stretched his body. His arms widespread.

“Going somewhere?” a voice asked.

Nathen turned to face the devil. “I’m going to Vatican City to take my revenge.”

“So soon?” the devil asked. “You haven’t learned the extent of your power.”

“I can learn that at a later time, right now I crave my revenge.”

“Very well!” the devil chuckled. “Take your vengeance on those you see fit then return to me.” “From this night forth, you will be my pupil and I will teach you my ways and you will be known to the world as Nithael, the Bloodmoon Dragon.”

“Yes master, so will it be.”

♀♀♀

ANGEL'S NEW CASE

Chapter One: Present day, 2000 years later

Sterlin Police Department was like a mad house. Phones rang off the hook. Officers scurried back and forth while suspects yelled from the holding cells in the back and the dispatchers jumped from call to call. The precinct was damn near chaotic every day. So, Angel came up with a method to zero out the mayhem around her. She'd plug in her ear buds, set up her I-Phone, get comfortable at her desk and let her playlist roll from track one. Alisha Keys was the first to sound off. ♫ A real man knows a real woman when he sees her. ♫ A woman's worth was the first song on Angel's playlist because she liked the message plus the melody helped her relax. Angel was seated at her desk reviewing the strange case she had been assigned when she noticed a shadow on her desk. She peeked up and then took out her earbuds. Detective Boyles was standing in front of her desk.

"Coffee? Miss. Spears?"

The slender woman asked holding up the pot in invitation. Angel looked at her cup. Her mug was almost empty, so she politely accepted Karen's offer.

"So, how's the case coming?" Boyles asked. She poured a stream of steaming hot coffee into Angel's cup. Angel picked up her cup and blew on it.
"Not so good." Angel said. "I've been working on this case for two days now and still, I have no leads, not even a clue."

Boyles poured herself a cup of coffee as well and then sat at her desk which was only a few feet away from the one they gave Angel to use. Her desk faced Angels so neither had to turn around.

"I heard it's a crazy case." Boyles said.

"Yeah, one of the few crazy cases Dillion has given me this month." Angel complained. Boyles chuckled.

"The only reason you get the difficult cases is because you're good with details. Not to mention, you graduated top of our class at the academy. I wouldn't be surprised if you made Captain next year." Angel smiled. She knew what Karen was getting at. Her career record had no blemishes and she closed almost all of her cases.

"Yeah, I know." Angel sighed. "I swear this case is beyond difficult. Something isn't right. Things don't add up and make sense. Normally, I could look at the evidence and the pieces would start to come together in my mind. You know, like a puzzle. Things would just lie in their rightful place, but this time, it seems the more I probe into the evidence the more it doesn't make sense. Hopefully, I'll know more once the DNA is concluded. I'm hoping to hear something from the Forensic Department today." Karen gave Angel a genuine smile then took a sip of her coffee. She didn't blow on it, so she made

a funny face when the coffee burned her mouth. Then the two burst out laughing.
"Well Bobby's out of town on business again, Karen said." Her tone of voice changed, and Angel caught it. "Now that my boys are off to college, I hate being in that big house all alone. Maybe you can come by sometime this week and we can go through the case together. It couldn't hurt to have a fresh pair of eyes." Karen explained.

"That sounds good." Angel lied. She preferred to work alone. She felt she did her best work when she could focus with no distractions. After the murder of her partner Steven Carter, Angel had no desire to be on cases with anybody, nor their family.

"Let me look at my schedule and I'll get back to you on that."

Angel let her off easy. She felt sorry for Karen because she didn't deserve what her husband was putting her through. Karen was a sweet woman, a good wife, and a great mother despite the fact Bobby was a known cheater throughout the precinct. He had been caught picking up prostitutes and seen with other women during his so-called business trips over the years. Karen knew her husband was a dog but for the sake of her dignity she'd never admit it. Instead she would come up with excuses for him and play dumb. Love can make you do that sometimes.

"Good morning Miss. Spears and Mrs. Boyles." A stern voice suddenly stated.

“Good Morning Captain Dillion.” The two women said almost in sync. Angel turned her chair to face the large uniformed Captain who stood in the doorway of his office.

“May I have a word with you Miss. Spears?” He asked.

“Sure Captain.” Angel sat her coffee on her desk and stepped into his office. Before the Captain said a word, Angel knew something was wrong. She could tell by his demeanor. He looked tense behind his desk.

“Should I sit down?” she asked.

“No, Angel this won’t take long. I just got off the phone with the commissioner. He was asking the question about the Sterlin Park cases and he was seeking answers that I couldn’t give him. Do you have any leads?”

Not yet Captain. I’m still waiting on the DNA reading to come back. We managed to get some semen and hair particles off the rape victim. I’m having them compared to the hairs that I found at the murder scene. Since both crimes happened at Sterlin Park only a day apart. I feel they are both connected. I feel the killer is stalking that area and that is a good chance that he’ll be back.” Dillion leaned back in his chair then thought for a moment.

“I hope so detective because the newspaper is having a field day with this. We need to catch this guy fast before the public and commissioner lose faith in our department. For now, you are relieved from all your previous cases. I want you to focus only on the cases similar to the Sterlin Park murder."

"That won't be necessary." Angel interjected.

"Oh, it's very necessary detective. I want this guy caught as soon as possible and you don't need any other cases to distract you. Oh, by the way, Dillion sat up and placed both hands on his desk, you have a meeting scheduled with Internal Affairs tomorrow. You need to be there by nine o' clock in the morning. So, make sure you're on time and please come dressed for the occasion. That means no blue jeans, t-shirts, or tennis shoes. You want to make a good impression."

"Do you know what it's about?" Angel asked. Steve had been dead for two years now. They didn't say much.

Dillion replied, "No, but I'm sure it has something to do with Steve so bring your "A" game."

"Thanks for the warning Captain!"

"No problem detective. Now get out there and find my killer!

♀♀

ZOE'S JOURNEY

Zoe sat silently in the passenger seat of his red Mercedes Benzes while his girl Rebecca drove down Highway 45. Sterlin City was their destination and they would be there in less than an hour. Zoe stared out the window looking down beyond the familiar scenery and the moving cars. The feeling of dread was upon him and it grew stronger with every passing moment. Zoe had vowed never to return to Sterling especially with a pending murder warrant too. He thought back to the argument he had with Rebecca and how she forced him to promise. Now he was forced to break that promise and the argument they had was furious. Rebecca tried to talk him out of going and Zoe hated to see her cry, but he knew a good leader always did what he had to do. Zoe was the leader of a gang called the G.M.C. which means "Get Money Crew." They started off with only five members. Him, his cousin Swade, Radar, Sweets, and Jeff and over the past four years with a little bit of dedication they had turned a small hood crew into a million-dollar drug operation. Swade was already known on the streets as a certified hustler and nigga not to be played with. He was Zoe's second in command. He had flourished the business while Zoe was out of state. Zoe handed down his orders over the phone using a code only the two of them knew or through his girl Rebecca who he sent down every other week to pick up his cut of the money. The song "Good Luck Charm" by Jagged Edge played on the radio and Rebecca turned it up.

"I bet you don't remember this song." she said.

"Yes I do. I dedicated this song to you." Zoe answered. She smiled.

"I was just checking." she said.

Zoe looked at Rebecca and smiled. Although she was sometimes crazy, she was fine as a motherfucka. A white girl built like a Stallion and super thick with all the assets a Black man loved in a woman. A pretty face, nice tits, and a fat round ass. She also had the intelligence to go with the package. She was a Georgetown College graduate who was now in the process of getting her lawyer license. A choice she had made after getting with Zoe. The two had been together for four years and Zoe liked almost everything about her. The way she smiled. How she tasted. The way her long brown hair touched her ass, but the quality he cherished the most was her loyalty. He knew without a doubt she would die before betraying him. True love! A concept he could never understand. In his mind to love anybody more than himself was stupidity and a sign of weakness and Zoe refused to be weak. He was a predator who easily used people for what he wanted, and Rebecca was no exception although he enjoyed her ways, he sometimes thought of her as weak and naïve. Deep down he knew he was a piece of shit that didn't deserve a woman like Rebecca. He just happened to get lucky. Zoe was a successful drug lord who loved the game. Unfortunately, fate was pulling him back to his old stomping ground. Although he loved his mansion in the suburbs of Wisconsin, he truly missed the hood and the people in it. Swade was killed in a shootout six months ago. So he started working with Swade's assistant Rob in order to keep the money flowing. Unfortunately, Rob wasn't the man for the job. Their business was losing too much money and the streets weren't respecting Rob like it did Swade. It turned out the death of Swade brought about a conflict with an up and growing rival gang called the Down Hill Gangsters who for some reason felt that Zoe's turf was up for grabs. This sparked an all-out war between the two gangs. The cost of war was taxing, and it was causing a drought to hit the streets. Zoe had to come down to appoint new leadership and discuss a truce with the D.H.G. leader. RIP or else they would lose more money and that was something he was not willing to do. Not even if it cost him his freedom.

♀♀♀

ANGEL FACES THE BOARD

Angel walked down the marble hall then stopped at the door that said Internal Affairs on the window. Their office had been on the third floor over the department. Angel looked at her watch. It was nine on the dot, so she walked in. The conference room was chilly and cold enough that Angel wished she had worn a sweater. She sat across from three of her fellow Officers with a thin wooden table between them. One of the Officers got up then set up a camcorder. Her fingers fumbled with the buttons. She looked at Angel and gave a polite smile. Perhaps to lighten the mood and Angel struggled to give it back. Angel knew who she was the moment she entered the room. Her dark hair and slim build were a dead giveaway. Agent Kathy Michells, also known as "The Butcher" among her fellow Officers. She was Internal Affairs rising star and a stunningly good investigator, probably as good as Angel. Michells positioned the camera then returned to her seat.

"My name is Kathy Michells. I'm in charge of this investigation. The gentleman next to me is Agent McBride. He will be assisting me, and you already know your Captain, Mr. Dillion. He insisted on being here, but you do have the right to be interviewed without him being present."

"It's fine. I don't have a problem with it." Angel consented.

"Ok, let's begin." Michells said.

"Can you state your name for the record?"

"Detective Angel Rose Spears."

"I'm investigating all allegations and conduct of your deceased partner Steve Carter. Are you aware of that?"

"Yes, I am."

"Have you ever witnessed Steve Carter doing anything illegal?"

"No Maam. Steve always stayed within the guidelines of the law."

"How long were you two partners Miss. Spears?"

"Three and a half years."

"And you never had seen Officer Carter do anything against the rules or illegal?"

"Now you're putting words in my mouth Mrs. Michells! I said he never broke the law in my presence. I said nothing about any rules."

"My apologies Miss. Spears."

"I guess I heard wrong. Did he ever break any rules around you?"

"Yes, minor things, like not wearing his seat belt, but nothing serious."

"Did you report these incidents?"

"No."

"Why not?"

"That would have been petty. Everyone has broken a rule at one time or another."

"Are you admitting you've broke the rules before?"

"I'm not admitting anything!"

Michells smiled. She knew she had gotten under Angel's skin which was her plan from the beginning. Just in case Angel came in with a script she wanted to say. You piss a person off and it's hard for them to remember what they planned on saying.

"How long have you been an Officer of the law Miss. Spears?"

"Five years."

"Is it true you made detective within a year and a half because you are extremely good at reading details and body language?"

"Yes, that is true."

"Yet you picked up nothing from your corrupted partner and you two worked together for three and a half years?"

"Steve wasn't corrupt!"

"Oh yes, he was Miss. Spears and we got the evidence to prove it. We know Detective Carter was not only a hit man for Zoe Johnson, he was also on his payroll and we believe he wasn't the only officer from this department on Zoe's pay list. How did you come to meet Zoe Johnson?"

"We were never formally introduced. Steve had his confidential informants and I had mine. We both dealt with community activists within our area. We learned by working together we could keep crime down and gain the trust of the people in the community. The first time I met with Mr. Johnson was the day I arrested him for Detective Carter's murder."

"Yeah, there are some questions on how you caught Zoe Johnson. According to him, you caught him coming out a girlfriend's house, gave him a chance to run, caught up with him, then beat him for resisting before you called it in."

"That wasn't his girlfriend's house. It was one of his crack houses and he got all those bruises from resisting."

"Well thank you for your cooperation Miss. Spears, but for reasons of our investigation, we are placing you on probation and ordering you to stay away from Zoe Johnson and anything has to do with his case."

"You're treating me like a dirty cop!" Angel interrupted.

"No mamm! It's just protocol. It's nothing personal."

"Protocol my ass." Angel snapped.

She slammed her hand against the table.

"Miss. Spears? Settle down!" Dillion growled.

He stood up and then walked over to Angel. He whispered something in her ear. Agent Michells couldn't hear it. Suddenly Angel settled down. Dillion was right. The situation was a set up. If she went off, they would take her badge and she would look guilty.

"Is there anything else?" Angel asked. Ready to go she stood up and looked down on the agents who stayed seated.

"Are we clear about the Zoe situation?" Michells asked.

"Crystal!" Angel replied.

"If we have any more questions we will get in touch. Thank you for coming." Agent Michells said.

She reached to shake Angel's hand, but Angel looked at her like she was crazy and then she turned and walked away. Angel headed out the door and Dillion followed behind her.

"What a Bitch!" She said.

Then Dillion started laughing. Angel walked to her desk and sat down. The interview with Internal Affairs went worse than she had thought. Michells had treated her more like a common criminal instead of a decent cop although her track record spoke for itself. Angel was a good cop who followed the rules and held the law and her police oath highly. Not once in the four years on the force had she been written up or in trouble with her Superiors. She worked hard to make a good name for herself and an honorable reputation. However, none of that seemed to matter to Internal Affairs. The only thing Michells seemed to care about was pinning Steve Carter's illegal dealings on her. Angel had a feeling they would try to bring her into Steve's affairs seeing she failed to turn him in. Although she knew Steve was dirty, he did a lot of good also and now that he was dead, Angel knew his family needed his insurance money, so she kept her mouth shut. Angel knew there was no way for them to prove she knew anything about Steve's activities, but now it was on her to prove her innocence or lose her job. She wasn't worried about jail time. She hadn't done anything illegal besides beat Zoe half to death, but that could only get her suspended if the precinct found out and it was her word against his. While her freedom was safe the security of her job was in jeopardy. Angel thought about her mother. She couldn't afford to lose her job while she was paying the bills for her Moms medical treatments. Angel's Mom was diagnosed with cervical cancer. Angel's Medical Insurance paid for the surgery, but the treatment was costing her a healthy sum that was coming directly out of her check. Losing her job was not an option. Not while her mother was still getting treatment. Angel cursed Steve for putting her in the predicament she was in, but he was dead now, so it would do her no good. She was left with only one solution. Find Peaches. Michells ordered Angel to stay away from Zoe, but they didn't say nothing about any other witnesses. Peaches was the stripper who witnessed the meeting between Zoe and three dirty cops. The meeting resulted in the murder of her partner Steve Carter, but the identity of the three crooked cops was still unknown. Peaches gave a description of the other two officers but none of them were a match to any Officers in the overall date base. Angel felt Peaches made the descriptions up because she was scared for her life and in all honesty, Angel didn't blame her. Who knows how far up the corruption went. Although Peaches gave a poor description of the Officers, her description of Zoe was right on the money. It was her statement that brought about Zoe's arrest two years ago, but like most drug lords, Zoe had high priced lawyers on standby. They greased all the right hands and got him out. Zoe wasn't locked up a day before he was out on bond. A week later he skipped town, and no one has seen him since. Unfortunately, Peaches disappeared around the time Zoe made bond and Angel wondered if she was dead, but she had no reason to contact the woman since Zoe was still on the run, however, things had changed. If Peaches couldn't help clear her name she may be able to point her to the right direction to get proof of her innocence. She typed Peaches real name into the computer and ran it threw the data base. Peaches last known address popped up. Angel wasted no time. She wrote the address down then headed to the parking lot. She had the rest of the day off, so she used the time to deal with her affairs. Angel got in her car and drove to Peaches last known address. The house was nicely painted with a fenced in garden. Angel got out of her car and walked to the door. They had a doorbell, but Angel knocked instead. An elderly woman answered the door. She explained that Peaches and her family moved away years ago around the time Zoe had been bonded out. Angel thanked the lady then walked to her car. A drop of rain hit her on top of her head. It began to rain so she decided to head home.

♀♀♀

DOMON ARRIVES

Chapter Two

Thunder flashed lighting up the night sky and rain poured down hard on the streets of Sterlin City. Domon watched the windshield from the back seat of the cab. The weather was furious. Arabic music played in the background. No doubt one of the cabby's CD's. He kept his eyes on the road. With one hand he turned up the volume. It blasted through the speakers. The music didn't bother Domon. He found it soothing. He particularly liked the flutes they used to create the rhythm. The cab pulled in front of a rundown looking hotel deep in the heart of the ghetto. The cabby put his car in park then looked over towards the back seat.

"Here we are my friend! The Regal. It's the cheapest hotel in the whole city, just like you asked." Domon gave the driver a polite smile then glanced at the meter. The cost was twenty-five dollars, but Domon handed him a fifty.

"Keep the change." Domon said. He took his luggage off the back seat then closed the cab door behind him. On his way to the lobby he bought a newspaper from the rusted newspaper machine. He placed the paper underneath his arm then walked into the building.

"Can I help you, a voice asked?" Domon looked over the counter and seen a young boy sitting in a large leather recliner. His little legs dangled in the seat.

"I would like to get a room." Domon replied. The kid scooted himself off the chair.

"I'll go get my daddy."

Domon watched the kid run into the back room. He could hear the boy talking to somebody. A few seconds later a chunky Black man entered the room. He wore khaki brown paints with a small T-Shirt. Domon could swear he had a chili stain on it.

"How can I help you?" The man asked. Rubbing the crust from his eyes. Clearly, the kid had woken him up from his sleep and he didn't look happy.

"I would like a room for a week." Domon said. "Do you rent by the day or just the hour? Either way is fine with me."

The owner said, "How will you be paying? Credit card or cash?"

“I’ll pay by cash.” Domon reached into his pocket and pulled out a big wad of bills. “Give me a room for one week.” He counted out seven hundred and placed it on the counter. “Here is seven hundred. It should cover my tab plus tips. If it’s not too much to ask, I don’t like to be disturbed.” The owner’s eyes lit up.

“Shit, for this kind of money that won’t be a problem.” He quickly picked up the money. He handed Domon the key. “You’re in room 306.” The owner said. He looked at the luggs on the floor two suitcases and a duffle bag. “If you need help with your luggage, I could have someone help you to your room.”

“That won’t be necessary.” Domon said.

The owner watched him pick up the entire luggage and enter the elevator. The guy was creepy he thought. The hotel didn’t have much business. Most of the rooms appeared to be empty and the floor was quiet. The light in the halls were dim and in need of changing, which was the way Domon preferred it, the cheaper the establishment, the less traffic to worry about. He walked into the room and hung his coat in the closet. He sat his bags on the closet floor and placed his brief case on the table walking back over to the closet. He opened one of the duffle bags and took out a pack of plastic cups along with a bottle of Wild Irish Rose. He opened the bottle and poured the thick red liquid into his cup. He pulled up a chair to the table and grabbed the newspaper from between his arm. He sat down and opened the newspaper. He was not surprised to see the article on the front page which read “POLICE STILL HAVE NO LEADS IN STERLING PARK MURDER INVESTIGATION.” Domon immediately put down the paper and pulled his laptop out of his briefcase. He turned the computer on and typed in a secret password and was instantly put through to a secure line. A familiar face appeared on the screen. It was Domon’s boss Cecil.

“How was your trip Domon?”

“Long and tiring.” Domon answered. He took a sip of his drink.

“I take it you read the paper?”

“Yeah, I just got done reading it.”

“We need this situation handled. Do whatever you need. Just please do it as clean and quiet as possible. Once you get their merchandise you know where to drop it off.”

“So, you want their heads?”

“That’s correct.”

“I’ll get on that tomorrow. Have a good night boss.”

“You too Domon.”

♀♀♀

NEW LEADS

Four case files of pictures and paperwork covered Angel's living room table. She has been studying the cases for over an hour. She walked into the kitchen to get another cup of coffee. She'd be up for a long time. Suddenly her second phone rang. She had gotten the phone strictly for her informants. So, she was sure to answer it on the first ring.

"Hello!" she spoke into the receiver.

"Is this Detective Spears?" A female asked.

"This is. How I can help you?"

The phone went silent for a couple of seconds.

"I don't know if you remember me." The lady stated.

"My name is Lizzy McDaniels. I worked for you a couple of times in the past."

Angel knew exactly who Lizzy was, a low-down junkie who would betray a friend in a minute.

"What can I do for you?" Angel asked.

"I was told you'll pay good money for any leads that bring about the arrest of Zoe Johnson."

"That's correct."

Lizzy exhaled.

"Well a friend of mine. I won't say her name, works for Zoe's crew. They hide money and drugs at her house. They pay her with drugs or money."

"So, your friend keeps a safe house for them?"

"Not only that, she gets the inside scoop because she's sleeping with one of Zoe's lieutenants. Word is Zoe has been in town for a day now. He back to put some things in order to attend a meeting."

"Why would Zoe come back?" Angel asked, skeptical about Lizzy's information.

Zoe was young, twenty-one to be exact, and far from dumb. There was no way he'd stroll back into town. Not with the murder of a cop hanging over his head along with the death penalty. Angel wondered if Lizzy was trying to set her up. Perhaps she was working for the anonymous dirty cops who attended the meeting with Zoe. The information definitely sounded too good to be true seeing that Angel spent the last four years arresting and pressuring members of Zoe's crew and got nothing. Now Lizzy popped up with a weak link in his organization. Chances like that were slim, but Angel heard Lizzy out.

“Word is Zoe lost over a million dollars since his cousin Swade got killed in a shootout with them D.M.G niggas. I’m sure you already knew Swade was the one running shit under Zoe’s authority. Since Swade’s death, both gangs have been at war.”

“I’m familiar with the turf war.” Angel concurred. She walked back over to the table and sat her cup down. Then she gave Lizzy her complete attention. I don’t see Zoe coming back to town to get revenge for a dead relative.”

“He’s not! The reason he is coming to town is to discuss a truce with the D.M.G. The leader RIP word on the street is the war is costing them manpower and money. My friend told me Zoe has lost over a hundred thousand in one week. That’s more than most people make in one year.”

“That’s a lot of money.” Angel agreed and it definitely seemed like a good reason to come back to her. “Do you know the location or time of the meeting?”

“No, but I know where Zoe going to be staying until the meeting.”

“And you’re sure he’ll be there?” Angel asked.

"Yeah, I'm positive. I looked Zoe up on the most wanted site and they only offered five hundred. That's not a lot of money for a cop killer."

"It's not." Angel agreed. She knew the price was low because Steve was suspected of being a dirty cop. "I'll tell you what. Give me the information. If it turns out to be good, then I will give you $1500. That's coming out of my personal pocket money." Lizzy paused for a moment as if she needed to think about the offer and Angel waited patiently for her answer.

"Sounds good to me." the woman said. She gave Angel the info and Angel wrote it down.

"I'll be in touch." Angel said. She saved the number to her phone.

"This is my cell number so you can call me anytime." Lizzy said eager to get the reward money.

"I'll call you in a few days." Angel replied.

She hung up the phone and smiled. Finally! Zoe had climbed up from under the rock he was hiding under and she would be there to haul him off to jail. Zoe barely left things in his operation. He calculated his moves carefully, however, this was a situation he couldn't foresee, and it seems that karma had led him straight into Angel's hands. At least that's how she hoped it would be. Angel hated Zoe. She would rather put a bullet in his head, a just revenge for murdering her partner.

However, her morals prevented her from doing so. Angel didn't have much time. She needed a plan. She couldn't bust Zoe herself, because internal affairs ordered her to stay away. If she reported, it she ran the risk of a dirty cop giving Zoe the heads up in order to protect their interests. She was in a bit of a bind and she couldn't trust any cop in her station. So, she decided to call an old friend from the Academy. It's been years since he hung out, but they kept in touch over the phone. Duke was the head of an undercover D.E.A. unit so she gave him a call.

♀♀

MARK'S RECKONING

Sunrise brought about a new day and Mark Walker a construction worker had just gotten in from a long night of partying. Deciding to take a bath he made his way to the bathroom. He turned on the tub of water and went into his bedroom to get a change of clothes. Walking back to the bathroom placed his stuff on the bathroom counter that included his t-shirt, a pair of his boxers, socks and Gun. He looked over at the tub. His water was ready. Walking over to the tub he stuck his finger in the water. The water was nice and hot just the way he liked it. Stripping out of his clothes he stepped into the tub. The water felt nice on his pale skin. Kicking his feet up he sank deeper into the tub. He could lay there forever. He relaxed his body and decided to rest his eyes just for a moment. A door slammed and Mark awoke from his slumber. Realizing someone was in the house he quickly turned up the water pressure in hopes of suppressing the sound of him getting out of the tub. He stepped out and grabbed a towel off the towel rack. It hung on the wall. He wrapped the towel tightly around his waist and grabbed the 38 off the counter. Letting his gun lead the way slowly opened the bathroom door and crept into his bedroom. Nothing looks out of the ordinary. He opened the bedroom door and headed down the hallway. Who's there? He yelled but there was no answer. He walked into the living room and looked around the room. It was empty. Nothing has been moved or changed. He began to wonder if he heard anything at all. Perhaps he had dreamed it but then it dawned on him that his bedroom door was closed. He had left it open when he came in and he hadn't been the one to shut it. He began searching the apartment with caution looking in all the closets and pulling back the curtains. He searched room to room. Finally, he worked his way back to his bedroom and there stood his intruder, a man in a black trench coat and a black top hat. Mark could see he had long hair, but his face was hidden by the shade of his hat.

"Put your hands up!" Mark demanded while the gun was pointed to the man chest. The intruder placed his hands above his head and Mark slowly stepped closer to see his face. "What are you doing in my house?" Mark asked but the intruder said nothing. "I'm not going to ask you again motherfucker!" Mark scolded.

"You won't have to."

Mark made a grave mistake when he stepped closer to see the man's face. The intruder quickly thrusted his hand forward knocking the gun from Mark's hand. Mark watched as the gun slip across the floor and stopped under his bed. He turned back to face the intruder and realized he was no longer there. Puzzled, he felt a hand top his shoulder. He quickly turned around. There stood the intruder holding a knife in his right hand.

"Nothing personal, he said, but business is business."

He grabbed Mark by the throat with one hand. He thrust the knife into Mark's stomach with the other. Mark could feel his warm blood as it gushed out of his body and at an extremely high rate. He struggled to get away but the more he fought, the tighter the intruder gripped his neck. Mark's eyes widened in a panic. He felt his chest start to ache as the air was being cut off from his lungs. The intruder watched as Mark's eyes suddenly changed from resistance to fear and then to acceptance.

"You are forgiven." the intruder said as he thrusted the knife further into Mark's chest piercing him through his heart.

He twisted the knife deeper into Mark's lifeless body. He could feel Mark's hot blood as it spurted from the wound and spilled over his fingers. He laid Mark face up on the floor then walked over to Mark's bed and pulled out a black duffle bag. He had planted it under the bed while Mark was in the tub. He opened the back and pulled out a hatchet with two medical zip lock bags. He walked back over to Marks body and began cutting his heart out. The knife slipped through Mark's tissue so easily it finished in no time. He took the heart and placed it into one of the medical bags and sealed it tightly. He set the bag next to the body. Then picked up his hatchet with one strong swing, he chopped off Mark's head.

"Tender meat!" He joked to himself.

He put Mark's head in the other bag then pulled his knife from the man's chest and licked the blade clean. He liked the taste of blood and the feeling he got from the hunt. He grabbed the towel from Mark's waist and wiped the blood off the knife handle and then placed it in a holster he had in the inner pocket of his coat. He walked to the kitchen sink and washed the blood off his hands. The blood covered the drain like a thick paint. He waited until the blood washed down then reached in his pocket to get his black leather gloves. He put the gloves on then grabbed the towel off the sink counter. He walked to the stove and cut on one of the eyes. He held the towel over the fire and waited until it burst into flames. He slung the burning rag into the sink. The towel burned away quickly. He wasted no time. He went to the bedroom and picked up the two plastic bags that lay next to his victim and placed them in two cooler boxes he had in his duffle bag. He zipped the bag up then headed to the front door. Killing was therapeutic to him and with that feeling he exited the front door and closed the door behind him as if nothing happened.

♀♀♀♀♀♀♀♀♀♀♀♀♀♀♀♀♀♀♀♀♀♀♀♀♀♀♀♀♀♀♀♀♀♀♀♀♀♀♀

ANGEL'S STAKE OUT

The clock on the dashboard glowed blue. It was 9:35pm and Angel's backup hadn't arrived. Where the fuck is he, she thought to herself? It wasn't like Duke to be late for a sting. Just then Duke knocked on her window.

Startled, she whispered, "You couldn't have called me first before you started knocking on my window like you cra cra? We are in the middle of a sting here." Angel unlocked the door and he jumped in the passenger seat.

"Sorry about that. Clearly, we're late," he said. "Everyone and everything is in place and they are waiting on my signal."

Angel then looked over to the house across the street. She'd been watching the house for the last two hours. Intel from her informant Lizzie was correct. Zoe had arrived at 7:30pm just like Ricky said.

"Did Zoe show up?" Duke asked making sure the raid was still a go.

"Yeah he pulled up in a red Mercedes-Benz. He had some woman driving and four of his guys pulled up in a car behind them. They all entered the house together. So, there are six from Zoe's crew."

"How many do you think are in the house?"

It's hard to say I haven't seen anybody leave the house and there hasn't been any traffic. My guess is just Zoe and his crew and maybe the owner of the house, but you never know."

Duke looked at Angel and smiled. "This should be a cakewalk. Just sit back and enjoy the show."

Duke hopped out of the car and crept to a van. A couple of cars away and in a few seconds later the place was swarming with DEA agents. Like ninjas, agents snuck toward the house. Angel couldn't believe how many agents were there. An agent accidentally triggered a motion detector on his pursuit to the front door. His step triggered the light and the place lit up like noon. Gunshots burst from within the house. The sound of automatic weapons filled the air as Duke and his team returned fire. Civilians in the house were no longer a priority. It was only getting their fugitive dead or alive. The agent in front of Duke caught a bullet to the chest but Duke kept on pushing.

"Get this door open!" He demanded ducking off behind a tree.

The Officers with the battering ram ran up the porch with no delay and gave the battering ram a good thrust. The door swung open and a swarm of AK bullets welcomed everyone. The bullets ripped through the agents vests as if they didn't even have one on. Their bodies rocked with every shot. Officers dropped like bowling pins falling one after another. Duke watched the skinny Officer fall down off the porch while the fat one slouched against a railing. Blood was pouring from his mouth profusely.

“Get these men some help.” Duke yelled.

He tossed a flash grenade in the door. It exploded with a blinding light. The gunmen struggled to see. That’s when Duke shot him in the chest. The agents put up a good fight, but they were being injured left and right although they were wearing body armor. The gunmen were using a special kind of ammo, the kind that tore through their swat gear. Duke figured the bullets were Teflon or perhaps some kind of military bullets. Whatever they were, he dreaded the outcome if the shootout continued.

“We need to get inside and take these men down.” he yelled.

Taking a chance, he rushed into the house. Angel saw that everything was going south fast. She grabbed the gun from her right holster and then bailed out the car. Stuck with two choices either to aid her compadres and face the music with Internal Affairs for being within 20 feet of Zoe or sit back and watch it all play out. Naturally she chose to aid her comrades. Angel slouched along the side of the car strategizing her next move. Angel knew the first half of Duke’s team was in the front while the other half advanced from the back. She chose to aid the team in the back. She was midstride when she noticed a basement window on the side of the house. The window was half-way open. It was almost too inviting. She wondered if someone had left it open on purpose. Perhaps when she stuck her head in she would get shot or maybe fate had it that someone had been careless. Whatever the answer was she decided to take the chance. She slid in the basement window and headed up the stairs. The room was empty. She headed up the stairs. Two gunmen were in the kitchen letting loose on the back door in an attempt to keep the agents out. They didn't see Angel sneaking up the stairway. This gave Angel an advantage. The men faced the back door, leaving their side open to Angel. Angel didn't want to kill the men, but the situation was far beyond taking them alive. Both shooters were in here sight.

Against her better judgment, she yelled out "Freeze!"

Her pistol aimed at one of the men, although there were two gunmen. She hoped that her 40 caliber was strong enough to cut through both men if need be. Angel reached for her spare gun and realized she left it in the car. Suddenly the gunmen made their moves. They aimed their guns in her direction forcing Angel to let off six shots. The closest man got it the worst. Seeing he was Angel's prime target he took in every bullet Angel sent and the man next to him caught two of the shots. He died immediately from a bullet to the heart. Angel ran over to the man laid out on the floor. Although he had been shot six times, he appeared to be breathing. She kicked the gun away from his hand and knelt down to check his pulse. Just then a group of agents stormed in the back door.

"We got him!" Duke called over the radio.

The news Angel had been waiting to hear for a long time. I.A's orders were clear. Stay away from Zoe and in part she had followed their rules, but unfortunately the shootout caused her to leave the car, which meant she was in trouble. Seeing she was already in trouble, she walked to the living room. Zoe and the blonde-haired chick laid face down on the floor. Two massive Officers stood over them, their guns aimed and ready. Angel noticed the cuffs on Zoe's wrists were very tight. She could tell because his hands looked blue.

"How did you get him?" surprised that he was still alive.

"Both of them were unarmed when we entered the house and they gave us no resistance." Duke answered.

Anger stirred within Angel. Four men were dead because of him and a handful of cops were injured during the course of his capture and now he was willingly giving up tucking his tail like a bitch despite his men who got killed trying to protect him. Angel looked down at Zoe. He returned her stare with a wicked smile taunting her. She paid it no mind. Two agents helped them both to their feet while a third agent read them their rights.

"You have the right to remain silent." The third agent said. Just then Duke tapped her on the shoulder.

"You should get back to the station." Duke said in a loud tone to be sure nobody else heard him. "I'll meet you there."

Angel gave Duke a nod then headed for her car. The bust was a success. There was no need for her to stick around. She hadn't counted on Zoe being alive once the shootout kicked off, but now she had a chance at clearing her name.

♀♀♀

STERLIN PARK

Chapter Three

The bright full moon provided plenty of light on the starless night while a spring wind blew a cool and gentle breeze within Sterlin Park. Angel walked along the long quiet trails of the park. Her mind was in deep thought. Nothing about the case made sense. The evidence pointed toward a suspect with incredible strength perhaps three times stronger than the average human. The forensics also came back inconclusive according to the forensic department. The blood splatter along with the hair particle turned out to be a positive match for a person with both wolf and human DNA, which she seemed impossible. Perhaps some Officer contaminated the evidence. Things like that did happen from time to time. Whatever the reason was she had no evidence, no clues, no suspects, and worst of all no leads. She began to wonder why Captain Dillion assigned her the crazy cases in the first place. Especially when he knew internal affairs was breathing down her neck. Perhaps he had more faith in her skills than she had in herself. Regardless of the reasons, she had promised him answers and she intended to keep that promise. Two of the crimes had happened around 9:30pm. The rape and the murder both occurred at Sterlin Park, and one victim gave a similar description of the suspect. He was big, hairy, and extremely strong. Both attacks were days apart which meant there was a good chance the suspect was really close and may strike again. Angel had a hunch the killer would be back if not to kill again, maybe looking around for his next victim or maybe revisiting the crime scene from afar. She figured the killer chose the park because it was easy for him or her to sit around and scout their victim. The killer could have watched the victim for hours and they wouldn't have noticed. A mistake most people make when they are too busy enjoying themselves and not paying attention to their surroundings. The illusion of safety and security. That's a luxury that only a civilian could have. Most cops lose that their first week on the force. Angel was no exception. She glanced at her wristwatch. The time was 8:30 PM. The night was still young, and she had plenty of time to waste. She sat on a nearby bench and watched as people walked by. One particular couple stood out from the rest. It was because they looked so happy. The couple passed by holding hands and smiling. They conversed with one another as if they didn't have a care in the world. She couldn't hear what the couple was talking about, but she could tell they were happy because they had the glow. The glow couples get when they are truly in love. Taken by the moment she thought about her life. Three years had passed. She hadn't been in a relationship and she was lonely. She had wanted to find her life partner, but she had to be honest with herself in her line of work. It was highly unlikely to have an honest faithful relationship because her job required a majority of her time. She had dreamed of the working husband, big house, and the white picket fence. Perhaps one or two little children to call her own, but the sad reality kicked in. The thing many people called love these days was an illusion. Very few people had found true love and her dream of finding her soulmate had vanished a long time ago and her acceptance of being alone had prevailed. She felt it was better to live alone then to live a lie with someone who was supposed to love her. She felt a bit of jealousy but quickly dismissed it. She looked at her watch and it read 10:30pm. She hadn't realized how much time had passed. She had been out there since 8:00pm and nothing seemed to be out of the ordinary. In fact the park was quiet and peaceful. Angel hoped for some clues or maybe more, but it seems she had run into a dead end or perhaps she was looking in the wrong spot. The landscape was huge, with many run along trails, trees, and bushes. Frustrated, she got off the bench and headed to the parking lot. On her way, she noticed a man sitting on a bench. Normally, she wouldn't have thought anything of it but it was the way he dressed that grabbed her attention. He wore a long black trench coat with a black top hat. The brim seemed to tilt forward which made it hard to see his face. He held a black cane in his right hand and a black brief case sat on the ground next to the bench. He watched a couple from afar. The couple was so into each other, so they didn't notice. Angel studied the stranger as she walked in his direction. The only people who did business in a park at night were drug dealers and pimps. He didn't look like a pimp. There was no doubt the cane he held was a concealed weapon. A sword disguised as a cane. Why he would need a sword was beyond her, but it was more reason to think of him as her suspect. Domon felt a stare from afar. He watched Angel from the corner of his eye and kept his other eye fixed on his targets. He had no idea who Angel was or why she was watching him, but he pegged her for a cop all though she was dressed casual with her white tennis shoes, blue jean pants, and a blue wind breaker jacket. The slight bulge under her jacket was a dead give-way although most people wouldn't have noticed it because it only poked an inch or two although it was his job to notice such things. The last thing he needed was interference from the police, so he decided to see if his hunch was correct. He waited until she got close enough to hear him then he asked.

"Excuse me, would you happen to know the time?"

Angel stopped and looked at her watch, "10:45pm she said."

She slipped both hands in her coat pocket trying not to look suspicious and held her small thirty-eight she had in one of her pockets. She pointed the gun on him through her coat.

"If you don't mind me asking, why would a beautiful woman such as yourself, be walking alone at night especially when there is a killer on the loose? Haven't you heart about the crimes that been happening around these parts?" Domon asked.

"I've heard but I'm sure I could hold my own if need be." Angel stated.

She looked down at Domon and tapped her holster to let him know she was strapped. Domon looked up at Angel and smiled. She finally had seen his face. He quickly put his head down realizing his mistake.

"I guess you're right." he said.

He stood up then grabbing his briefcase. "Just be careful." he warned.

Angel gave him a nod then said, "You too."

She watched as Domon turned and walked away. From the way he talked he knew something or perhaps he was up to something. Being herself didn't cut it. Maybe she needed to take a more feminine approach.

"Wait!" Angel called calmly.

Domon turned to face her, "What's up?" he asked?

"I never got your name." Angel said as if she was interested in him.

"My name is Mary." she said, putting out her hand.

Domon took it and kissed the back of her hand like the old gentleman used to do in the old days. Caught off guard, Angel tried to retrieve her hand, but it happened to fast.

"My name is Aaron." he said with a smile. Although he knew Angel was lying about her name by the sound of her heartbeat, he played along with it.

“Do you come here often?” Angel asked? She already knew the answer because she strolled the park on the regular and this was her first time seeing Domon.

“No, this is my first time coming to this park.” Domon answered. He knew Angel was testing him.

“I don’t mean to sound nosey, but you asked me a personal question so now I’m asking you one. What brought you out to this park this night knowing that a killer is on the loose?” Angel said.

Domon studied her for a second. Her demeanor was calm and convincing. He knew she was trying to study him and get as much information as possible. He was surprised how good she was at it. He could have been fooled if he didn’t know better.

“Well, this is kind of embarrassing for me to say, but I’ll tell you anyways. I was supposed to meet my date here tonight, but it seems she stood me up.”

“That’s awful!” Angel said. Her tone was sympathetic. Domon looked over to his targets. The couple had gotten away.

“I really must be going.” he said. Hoping he would catch up with his targets. “Here’s my card.” Domon said. “Maybe we can get together some time, perhaps go out for coffee or something?” Angel took the card and smiled.

“That would be nice.” she said.

Domon turned around and walked away and Angel looked at the card. It said Aaron Kennedy, Attorney at Law. How convenient was that? Angel thought to herself her only suspect was a criminal attorney. She looked ahead to find Domon, but it was like he vanished. He was nowhere in sight. She sensed he was in a rush and eager to get somewhere. Her plan was to give him some distance and then follow him but that was no longer an option. Damn, he’s fast, she thought to herself as she made her way to the parking lot. At least I have his number. I’ll start my investigation tomorrow.

♀♀

ZOE IN THE COUNTY

"Damn man! Another day of this bullshit! Sometimes I wish I would've fought back." Zoe complained. He hopped off the top bunk. He walked over to the toilet and took a leak. He was now in Morgan County jail being held without bond and today was the second day.

"If you would've fought back, you'd be dead right now." his Bunkie said. "Look on the bright side, at least you got away with your life. Plus, today is my birthday and you are the only one I got to celebrate it with."

Ralph pulled a garbage bag from under his bunk. It contained two gallons of hooch. Prison wine. Zoe seen the bag and knew what it was off top. Zoe smiled, then handed Ralph his cup. Ralph dumped his cup, and then gave it back.

"You got to take the first cup to the head." he said, downing his first cup also.

The cell was small, so the toilet wasn't that far from the bed. Zoe sat on the toilet and waited for his refill. Ralph handed Zoe his cup. It was filled to the brim. He looked over to Ralph's cup and so was his. He smiled to himself. Ralph was trying to get him fucked up. Ralph was an O.G. from the hood known for not taking no shit. He was rumored to have beaten a man to death with his bare hands over five dollars. He really wanted his five-dollar foot long from Subway. Zoe had heard his name ringing a few times in the streets, but he thought of him more as a hot head and there was no room for hot heads in his organization and therefore, he didn't reach for him.

"How long have you been locked up. I was wondering why I ain't heard shit about you in the streets?"

"Two years. I'm fighting a murder and attempted murder, the O.G. said, but it is what it is! We are not going to discuss that today. It's time to celebrate."

Within a few hours they drunk at least five cups a piece and Zoe was feeling good and so was Ralph.

"This is the last cup."

Ralph handed Zoe a refill cup but being in the state of mind that Zoe was in, he didn't notice the pills that were melting at the bottom. Ralph put in his cup pills called Seroquel. A pill that helps you sleep, but if you took too many of them, you'd fuck around and never wake up. Ralph put five of them in Zoe's cup.

"I appreciate you celebrating my birthday with me homeboy." Ralph said.

Slowly, as he watched Zoe finish his cup, the two talked for about another fifteen minutes then Zoe faded out. Ralph smiled and went back to work. He grabbed two bedsheets and ripped them up. He braided the strings together making a rope. He fed it through the vent that was providing air into the cell from the ceiling. He tugged on the vent to be sure it would support the weight of a body. It did. So, he wrapped the other end around Zoe's neck and positioned him so that he wouldn't get loose, because he's gonna fight. Ralph began to pull Zoe up to the ceiling and his body came alive. Zoe's hands reached for his neck, not realizing what was happening. Ralph pulled harder. Zoe's head hit the vent. His body continued to struggle fighting for his life. Ralph tied the rope to the window, then cut the light out. It took Zoe five minutes to finally stop fighting and die. Ralph hit the button.

"Yeah!" The Correctional Officer came over the speaker.

"My celly! He hung himself! Hurry up!"

The section lights came on and a group of Correctional Officers rushed into Ralph's cell.

"How did this happen?" they asked.

Ralph responded with a serious stare.

"I woke up and he was hanging. I want no part of this."

The Officers took Ralph's mattress and put him in a different cell. Ralph made his bed, and then laid down with a smile. Detective Jinsend, the head detective of his murder cases, would make those cases disappear tomorrow.

DANGER IN STERLING PARK

Chapter Four

John and Sarah Wentfield strolled along Sterlin Park trails. They were engulfed in deep conversation when they spotted a fur like creature standing in some wooded area on the outskirts of the park. Unable to make out what the creature was, they stood in shock and afraid to make any sudden moves.

"Back away, slowly!" John whispered to Sarah.
"One step, at a time!" he said.

Sarah scared out of her mind struggled to mimic John's footsteps, but she did a good job keeping up one step at a time. The creature watched as its prey backed away. Its eyes zeroed in on Sarah. His senses heightened to the point that her scent drove him crazy, stirring up a fire in its loins. Giving off a light growl, it ran full force at the couple. Panicking, the couple turned to run away, but the creature was too fast. In an instant, it was right behind them. It raised one hand and smacked John on the back of his head. The blow made a cracking sound and spun John's body in the air and knocked him unconscious. Sarah glanced back to see her beloved lying face down in the grass, a puddle of blood surrounding his face, letting out a loud cry of pain. She screamed for dear life.

"Help! Help! Help me please!"

At that moment she felt the warmth of the creature's breath on the back of her neck and suddenly, she was knocked unconscious. Sarah awoke with tiny pains from scratches and bruises that she was accumulating by being drug by the creature. She screamed as loud as she could, hoping someone would save her, but the creature kept on dragging her. It gripped tightly around her ankle. It dragged her body across the large grass field of the park and then made its way into the large forest area of the park, dragging her deep within the forest. It let go of her ankle and grabbed her by the neck, pinning her small body against a large tree. With its claw like fingers, it slashed at Sarah's blue and white flower dress. The fabric ripped like a razor thin paper leaving Sarah's breasts exposed. With its doglike nose, it sniffed on Sarah and stopped at her white cotton panties. The beast snatched her panties off. Her bloody maxi pad fell to the ground. It sniffed in between her legs then gave out a low grunt. It slid her back and forth against the tree getting her in the right position. The beast gave off a loud grunt. It's Wolfhood starting to get erected. Sarah screamed frantically realizing what the beast was about to do. She could see its long harry pecker expanding from its body.

"Oh no! Oh God, No!" Then a scream.

The parking lot was nearly empty except for Angel's car, another car, and the small yellow Grand Am with the foggy windows that rocked back and forth from some horny couple who clearly couldn't find a room. Angel had just made it to her car when she heard the screams of what sounded like a female. She grabbed her 40 caliber out of her holster and headed in the direction of the screams which took her deep into the woods into a place where normal people wouldn't go at night. She quickly made her way past the trees and through the bushes. Very few rays of light went through the leaf covered branches which covered up the moons light. She finally made it to the source of the cries and she pointed her gun at the attacker's back. The forest was very dark. This made it hard for Angel to get a clear identification of the attacker. She stepped closer and seen a huge man holding a woman against a tree. He appeared to have on some kind of fur coat. With one hand he held the woman's body off the ground.

"Freeze! Angel yelled! Take your hands off the woman now!" she demanded.

The suspect stopped as if complying with her wishes. He dropped the woman. Her body gave off a slight thump when she hit the dirt. He turned around to face Angel and she froze at the sight of the thing. It definitely wasn't human. It was big like a bear but its features were that of a crossbreed of a human and a canine. Its eyes were the color of hot coals and its fur black like soot. Oh shit! Angel thought to herself. Struggling to remain calm, she took a few steps back. Trying to keep her composure, but her body wouldn't comply. She felt her body shaking terribly as if it had a mind of its own. She gripped her gun tightly hoping it wouldn't fall from her sweaty palms. She wanted to shoot but she was afraid that she would shoot the victim. The beast watched Angel like a snake watches its prey. It could smell the fear coming off her, which gave it a hint of satisfaction, but that was nothing compared to the anger it felt from Angel disturbing his fun time. It started at her full force. Angel managed to let off three shots hitting the beast once in the chest and twice in the head. The beast stumbled back from the shots then fell backwards to the ground. Angel starred at the beast in disbelief as it lay motionless on the ground. What type of animal is this, she thought to herself. Cautiously, she walked up to the beast to get a closer look. Her gun pointed at its head. She watched to see if its chest was still moving, but it was hard to tell. It didn't appear to be breathing, nor did it budge in any way. She gave the area a quick scan looking for the lady who had been attacked, but the lady had already run away. Angel wasn't surprised. She may have done the same if she was her. She reached for her cell phone and realized she had left it in her car. Somewhat relieved for a reason to get out of the woods, she headed to her car. She hurried to get out of the woods. The last thing she needed was another one of those creatures attacking her in the dark. She prayed that she could make it to the parking lot where sunlight was at least to have a better chance and to get better ammunition. At least that's what she thought. A twig broke behind her, and she quickly turned around and there stood the beast. She managed to get off one shot which landed in the beast just for the creature not to even seem to sweat it. It slapped the gun out of Angel's hand and then smacked her to the ground. Angel looked up with sheer fear in her eyes, accepting what was to come next. The beast raised his hand and Angel closed her eyes, preparing for the blow. The beast let out a loud cry and Angel opened her eyes and seen a large silver arrow sticking out of the creature's chest. Angel watched as the beast stumbled and fell to the ground. Then she heard a voice asking from the shadows...

"Are you okay? Domon asked.

"Yes!" Angel replied, coughing repeatedly. Domon stepped from behind a tree with the crossbow gripped tightly in his hand.

"Can you help me to my car?" Angel asked as she leaned on a tree as she struggled to get to her feet.

"I told you it was dangerous out here!" Domon teased, and Angel gave him a dirty look.

He took Angel by her arm and placed it around his neck, and he grabbed her legs and lifted her up, holding Angel firmly. He carried her through the woods. He carried her as a man would carry his wife over the threshold on their wedding day. It had been a long time since Angel had been held. Domon's arms were strong yet soft. He even smelled good to. Instead of putting up a fight about being carried, she'd let him get away with it, just this one time. She just laid back and enjoyed it.

♀♀

JUSTIN RAY'S VISION

Chapter Five

Images played in Justin Rays mind like a movie projector. He struggled to escape the horrific dream, but his body wouldn't allow him to awake. Paralyzed in his own skin by an unknown entity, he was forced to watch the gruesome images of countless men, women, and children being torn apart and slaughtered by an ungodly creature. A feminine voice spoke in the background.

"Find the priesthood of Yahoel!" the voice instructed. "You have now witnessed its carnage. The Blood Moon Dragon must be destroyed. Let this be a warning to Rome and the entire world." It warned.

Justin woke up at that moment. He wiped the sweat off his forehead, but his entire body was drenched in sweat. He took a moment to gather his thoughts, but there was no doubt that he experienced a prophetic vision, but why? He was no longer a Cardinal. He gave up the cloth seven years ago. Now his life was about golf, booze, and women which are the exact opposite of a priest's life. His job as a college professor was sometimes stressful but he enjoyed teaching religion and history to the curious minds in his class. The voice told him to find the priesthood of Yahoel. The problem was that religion had been extinct for over 2000 years. At least that's what the archaeologists believed. Perhaps they still existed. Maybe they were some secret group or maybe they went underground for some reason. Whatever the case, there is only one place he could find the answers. Vatican library archives. Unfortunately, he no longer had access since he walked away from the church. Justin knew he would have to plea for an audience with the Vatican Council and once doing so, explain his vision and hopefully they would grant him permission to view the archives. He had hoped that others had received the same vision. Therefore, it wouldn't be hard to convince the Council, but he could only hope.

☥☥☥

STERLING PARK-AM I CRAZY?

Officer Terrence Lenwood was the first to arrive on the scene and Angel sat nervously on a curb. Her body was shaking beyond her control.

"Are you okay?" Lenwood asked.

"Yeah, I'm okay. I was attacked by some kind of wild animal."

"What kind of animal?"

"I don't know!" Angel snapped. Standing up from the curb, she could tell that Lenwood was deeply concerned. "I'm sorry." she said.

"It's nothing Angel. You've been through a lot tonight. What happened to the beast?"

"It's dead." Angel explained. "A man killed it."

"What man?" Lenwood asked.

"A suspect that I was investigating, He killed it. Then he helped me out of the woods." Angel replied. She didn't want to tell anyone that the man had carried her out of the woods. Lenwood looked around the parking lot and nobody was there except for the two of them.

“Where is he now?” Lenwood asked?

“He said he was going back into the woods to make sure that the beast was dead, but I don’t think he is coming back out.”

Angel walked over to her car and opened her trunk.

“You’re going to need a bigger gun.” she said.

She grabbed her 12-gauge pump shot gun. Lenwood nodded and grabbed a Mossberg pump he had in between the seats of his squad car.

“Is this big enough?” He asked.

“Yeah.” Angel said.

At that moment, two ambulances arrived along with a group of squad cars. Two paramedics exited the truck and rushed over to Angel and Lenwood.

“Our patient said her fiancé is lying in the middle of the park and in need of medical assistance.” one of the paramedics said.

“We haven’t checked the park yet.” Lenwood said. “I just got here.”

Angel looked at the woman who sat in the back of the ambulance. She recognized her. It was the woman from the couple she had noticed earlier in the park. The couple she had gotten jealous over.

"Follow me." Angel said. "I will escort you through the park."

Angel led the medics quickly to the park. Her stomach was tied in knots. She hoped the husband was still alive. The woman would be crushed if he wasn't. She felt so bad for envying them. The man laid face down in a puddle of blood. His face submerged.

One medic placed a finger on his wrist and stated, "He has a pulse, but it's weak."

"Let's get him into the truck." the other medic said.

They laid the stretcher next to the victim and placed the man on the stretcher. Angel watched another ambulance pull up and they put the man on the stretcher in the truck.

"Do we have the okay to leave?" the paramedic asked. "This man needs to be treated at a hospital."

Angel glanced around the crime scene then gave them the okay to leave. The way she seen it, it was an open and closed case. Clearly, the man had been attacked by some kind of wild creature and it was the same one that also attacked her. What other questions she may have, she would get them from the victim's wife. The crime scene forensics had arrived. She had them put down some flags around the crime scene. She walked back to the parking lot. The place was swarming. She noticed the ambulance was still there. She walked to her car and got her note pad and radio then headed to the ambulance. As she got closer, she could see the woman shaking and crying in the back of the truck. Her head had been wrapped in white bandages. It stopped below her eyebrows. Her minor cuts were covered with Band-Aids.

"Hi. I'm Detective Angel Spears. I'll be the one investigating you and your husband's case." The woman looked up at Angel with tears in her eyes.

"Is he all right?" She asked.

"Yes, he is all right and I believe he's going to make it. The paramedics have taken him to the hospital already." The lady's eyes displayed both bitterness and joy.

"I want to see my husband." She said.

She stepped down out of the ambulance. A medic grabbed her by the arm and attempted to stop her, but she snatched her arm away.

"Am I under arrest?" the woman asked Angel.

“No!” Angel replied.

“I’m going to be with my husband.” the woman said.
Angel wasn’t going to stand in her way.

“I’ll be in touch.” Angel said.

Angel watched the woman get in her car then speed out of the parking lot. Although it was illegal, there was nothing she could do. She wasn’t about to chase her down and give her a speeding ticket. A rookie walked up to Angel.

“Excuse me, Miss Spears?” “You are wanted at the crime scene.”

Angel rushed over to the crime scene. Maybe they had figured out the species of the creature that attacked her. She had never seen anything like it. She knew it had been responsible for the rape and murder and now the attempted murder, but she wouldn’t know for sure until she found more DNA and retested the DNA she already had. Three homicide detectives studied the crime scene and the creature lay a few feet away. Its body covered by a sheet.

“You may want to recant your statements.” Lenwood said taking Angel by the arm. He pulled Angel off to the side, but one of the detectives saw him.

“Over here Miss Spears.” The detective said.

Angel walked over to the three men standing by the body. They uncovered the body and there laid a thin man without a head, a silver arrow to his chest.

“I don’t understand!” Angel said staring at the headless white male. “I was attacked by some kind of beast animal.”

“Are you sure your attacker was an animal? It is dark out here? The fat detective asked.

“How did this guy get out here?”

“Someone killed him and took his head!”
“I told you, I don’t know how we got here!” Angel said. “Do you think it’s a coincidence that me and the victim both seen the same creature?”

“That is strange.” Lenwood said. “Let’s just gather all the evidence together and we can sort it out later.” Lenwood looked over at the body then said “Angel? You need to find the guy who did this before Internal Affairs gets wind of this situation.”

Angel could tell that Lenwood had her back and she was grateful.

“Yeah! I’m in a bit of a mess. My career may be over or worse. I’ll end up in jail.”

"I'll handle the investigations." Lenwood said. "You go home and get some rest and get your thoughts together. Don't worry about it. I got you Angel. Remember from this moment on every move you make counts."

"Thanks Lenwood."

Angel patted him on the shoulder struggling to keep a calm face but deep inside she knew the situation was bad and headed to her car. Angel found herself in the middle of a shit storm with no idea how she got there. Everything had happened so fast. Even if she proved to internal affairs that she wasn't dirty, how would she explain being on the scene?

♀♀

MEETING WITH CAPTAIN DILLION

Chapter Six

Domon scratched off another name from his list, two down, three more people to go. He knew Mark and Carlos would be easy because they weren't the pack type. They were loners who preferred to be by themselves, but Anthon and the others would be much harder. They had money with a lot of skilled paid security plus they stayed in the public eye. Domon walked into the hotel room and looked at the clock. It was midnight. He had nine hours before his meeting with Capt. Dillion. He had no idea what the meeting would be about. He just knew he was ordered to be there by his superiors. He took his new obtained head and put it in a special lockbox cooler next to the other head. Domon preferred the jobs where he really had no contact with people other than his target. He could slip in and out of the city without being noticed, but this time he was denied that luxury. Anthon and his troops had made number one on the Councils to deal with list and Domon was there to execute their sentence. He plugged the second lock box cooler in the wall. He walked over to the kitchen and took a small plastic bag out of the refrigerator. He reached into the bag and pulled out the heart. He placed it into the blender. It turned the small heart muscle into a slushy. Then he poured his nutritious drink into a cup. He grabbed his briefcase and placed it on the counter. Flipping to the right combination, it unlocked. He opened the case and powered up his laptop. Domon typed in his password and immediately a face popped up on the screen.

"What is the status?" The man asked.

"Two down. Three to go! They are on ice. I'll drop them off at the safe house tomorrow."

"So, your mission is coming along gracefully?"

"That is correct."

"I never doubted you Domon."

"Thank you sir!"

"Are you ready for the meeting?"

"Yes sir!"

"Dillion is a good friend of mine."

"If you don't mind me asking, what will our meeting be about?"

“You will see when you get there Domon. Anthon and his men are difficult opponents. They want to expose our kind to the humans. Be sure not to blow your cover.”

“I won’t sir.”

“Have a good night.”

“You too Domon.”

Domon shut the computer down and downed his protein drink. He left the kitchen counter and walked over to the bed. He picked up the remote up off the small nightstand. He began flipping through the channels and that’s when he seen it. Breaking news on the television in all capital letters that stated;

“MAN FOUND BEHEADED IN PARK. SUSPECT WAS WEARING A BLACK HAT AND TRENCH COAT. THE SUSPECT WAS SAID TO BE A MALE WITH LONG BLACK SHOULDER LENGTH HAIR. HEIGHT ABOUT 5”4 WITH BROWN EYES AND HIGH CHEEK BONES. HE IS BELIEVED TO BETWEEN THE AGES OF 28 TO 34. Although our sketch is not an exact match, He is believed to look something like this.”

Domon starred at the sketch. Although it wasn’t accurate, it was enough for the public to identify. It did come fairly close. Damn! She’s good. Domon thought to himself. In the midst of all that happening, she still managed to get a close look at his face. He definitely would have to change the way he dressed. No more easy to conceal weapons. A problem, but something he had to deal with. Ironically, in just a couple of hours he will walk into the Sterlin Police Station to see Captain Dillion. He was sure none of the Officers would recognize him at the police station, but the officer he knew as Mary would not only point out that he was the one at the park, she may try to arrest him for the murder. If Mary recognized him, things could get ugly. If he got arrested, it would be on him to get himself out. Nothing could trace back to the Council. He shook his head and pushed the worries out of his mind. What has the Council got me into?

♀♀♀

ANTHON'S OFFICE

Anthon laid back in his comfortable recliner. His legs kicked back on his desk. He stared at the ceiling of the expensive office and smiled. Business was good, and this year, is going to be his biggest cash cow ever. They had sold more tickets and bids than in previous years. He didn't expect the word to get around so quickly. People were willing to pay ridiculous amounts of money to reserve one of the thirty seats available. His entertainment would be well worth it. Never leave the customer unsatisfied was his motto. That way of thinking had gotten him rich. He thought back to the time when he was a bum with no money and worried where he would find his next meal. He worked hard for his money indulging in every hustle he could legal or illegal. He invested that money in a landscaping business and never looked back. He was now a member of the Fortune 500, and a successful businessman who had the world eating out of his hands. The phone rang and he picked it up. He knew it was his secretary.

"Yes, Sarah?"

"Sorry to disturb you, Mr. Parker, but Frank Willcon is here to see you."

"Okay. See him in."

Anthon took his feet off the desk, then propped himself up on the desk to look professional. That's when Frank walked in.

"I called your phone, but I kept getting the voicemail." Frank said.

"Sorry, I didn't want to be disturbed."

"Well this is very important, and I couldn't reach you."

"What is it Frank?"

"Someone killed Mark. His body was discovered yesterday."

"That's no surprise." Anthon said coldly. Mark was wild, short tempered, and had lots of enemies. "It was bound to happen sooner or later."

"That's true, but the cops found his body without his head and heart. I am not trying to panic you, but it sounds like the Council to me."

"It does." Anthon agreed.

He took a second to think and Frank broke the silence.

"We never sponsored a rave with the order so close on our trail. Maybe we should cancel the rave. Pick up and go why we got the chance." Anthon looked at Frank like he was crazy.

"Too much money is wrapped up into this project." Anthon explained. "The rave must go on."

"But?"

"No buts Frank. You heard what I said. I don't want to hear any talk about canceling the rave again. If anything, let's figure out a way to make these go by smoothly, am I clear?"

"Yes, boss! Loud and clear!"

Frank stood there for a moment as if he had something to say, but he exited the office. He closed the door behind him. He took out his cell phone and dialed the number.

"Willcons Incorporated! Can I help you?" An operator asked.

"This is Frank, put me through to Jake, Please!"

"One second sir."

"This is Jake. What can I do for you sir?"

"Everything is a go. Send the e-mail."

"One-minute sir. The emails have been sent. Is there anything else?"

"That will be all. Have a nice day Jake."

"You too Frank."

Frank hung up the phone and paused for a minute. Deep down he felt Anthon had made the wrong call but who was he to second guess Anthon. It was Anthon who took him off the street and got him clean when he was a junkie. It was because of Anthon he was now rich. Frank knew the risks when he teamed up with Anthon and his illegal rave parties. So how could he say no to the man who is not only his best friend, but took him from nothing and made him something? Frank no longer liked the raves, but he was in it till the end because Anthon needed him to be. His views on humans had changed over the years. He became sympathetic towards them. Poor kids! He thought to himself. At that moment some teen received an anonymous email.

♀♀♀

JUSTIN IN ROME

Chapter Seven

It didn't take much for Justin to schedule a meeting with the Cardinal. One phone call to an old friend in the Vatican, and the meeting was set. Unfortunately, he couldn't have the meeting in the US. He had to fly to Rome to attend which was a major inconvenience for him, seeing he didn't have much money and was living off a teacher's pay. A flight to come to Rome and back will cost a nice amount of money. Not to mention, the hotel and car expenses. He took flight. It was surprisingly relaxing because it gave him time to gather his thoughts. He jotted them down in a small notebook. The vision was vivid. He had no problem writing down the images, but he wasn't sure how he was going to present things. A rental car was left in the airport parking lot, so he got the keys from a worker at the front desk. He walked to the parking lot and hit the button on his keychain and the car let off a beeping sound. It was a 2016 blue Grand Am. He opened the door and got in. The car was much nicer than the 1997 Oldsmobile he drove back home. The church he would be meeting in wasn't far away. He made it there in twenty minutes. He pulled into the church parking lot and spotted his escort standing at the church door. Justin emptied his pockets and put his cell phone in the glove compartment. He knew security was very strict when dealing with cardinals. He got out of the car and walked to the door.

"Mr. Ray?" The priest asked.

"I am!"

"I am Father Philip. I will be escorting you to the meeting hall. I'm sure you already know, no phones, no cameras, no tape recorders, or weapons are allowed. We do this for security purposes."

"I am aware." Justin said. "I left all of my belongings in the car." The priest nodded.

"Let's get going then!"

The two walked into the church where security personnel guarded the door. One guard patted them down then sent them to the other guard who used a hand-held metal detector to screen him.

"There clean." One guard said to the other. He gave the priest a nod.

"You guys can go through."

"Follow me." Philip said, as he led Justin to the church halls and up a flight of stairs.

They walked down another long hall, and then they entered a wooden door that led into a large room decorated with silk curtains and a glistening marble floor. Expensive paintings hung on the wall and most of them resembled moments from the Bible. The picture that stood out the most to Justin was a painting of Adam and Eve in the Garden of Eden. The serpent lurked in the bushes. A wooden chair was in the middle of the room. It faced the small stage where three cardinals sat in big plush chairs. Justin looked at the three cardinals. One middle-aged and the others looked no older than twenty-three years old.

"Have a seat." The older Cardinal said. Justin sat down. He looked up at the three men.

"How can we help you?" The younger Cardinal asked. The others stood quiet.

"First off, thank you for seeing me. I know you are all very busy. As you know, I too was a Cardinal before I became a history and religion teacher. The reason I'm here is because I had a horrible vision and warning. I was told to find the priest of Yahoel."

"Told by whom?" The older Cardinal asked now irritated thinking the meeting had been a waste of his time.

"I'm not sure." Justin replied. "But I believe it was an angel." Justin took the notebook out of his pocket. "I wrote the details down in this notebook." He handed the small book to the younger looking Cardinal, who quickly passed it to the middle-aged Cardinal who looked it over in silence.

"Why would an angel instruct you to find the priesthood of Yahoel?" The young Cardinal asked. "They have been extinct for over 2000 years."

"I don't know. Perhaps the sect is still around."

The Cardinals looked at one another as if surprised to Justin's answer. They whispered back and forth to each other. Unfortunately, Justin could not hear what they were saying. The older Cardinals demeanor had completely changed once he read the notebook. He appeared to be passionate about what he was saying, but the younger two cardinals didn't seem to be interested.

"To be clear, you are asking for permission to obtain access to our library and archives?" The older Cardinal asked.

"That is correct."

The Cardinals looked at each other then asked Justin to leave the room so they could deliberate. Justin gave them a polite smile, nodded, and stepped into the hallway. Father Philip stayed in the room but closed the door behind him. Justin knew it was to prevent him from hearing what they were saying. A few minutes passed and

Philip opened the door and asked us to come in. The young Cardinal handed Justin the notebook.

"After deliberating, your vision may have some merit, but not enough to give you access to our library. The vote was 2 to 1 in favor of no, but we will contact you if something new comes up to verify your vision. May God bless you Mr. Ray."

Justin couldn't believe his ears. Deep down, he had hoped everything would work out the way he needed it to. Now he was denied entry to the only place they could give him the information he needed. He thought he had the force of God behind him, but perhaps he was wrong. He thanked the Cardinals for their time, then headed for his car. He had reached the parking lot when a voice called out. He turned around to see Father Philip who reached to shake his hand. In the palm of his hand was a note.

"Look at it once you get into your car." he said. "There is surveillance everywhere."

Justin gave him a quick nod and got into his car. He looked around the parking lot to make sure nobody saw him. He opened up the paper. It was a note from the older Cardinal.

It said, "I may be able to help. Meet me at my apartment at 7:00p.m. Here's my address. 1706 Pennsylvania Ave. Come alone."

♀♀♀

THE RAVE

Chapter Eight

Sunset drew near and music blasted from the large concert speakers within the tremendous abandoned factory that the anonymous host chose to have his concert. Charlie had a bad feeling about going to a rave whose location was anonymous. The way he seen it, a concert who wouldn't disclose their whereabouts until the last minute had to be illegal, especially if they allowed underage drinking. Which he was sure would be there along with every other drug under the sun. Charlie understood why the sponsor wanted to remain anonymous. No one wants to get caught with a concert full of teens that were underage drinking and doing drugs. But, why spend so much money on a party he would make actually nothing off of? Everything had been free. The drinks were free, the food was free, and the parking was even free. None of it made sense. To him, what did make sense was there was a catch to it. Charlie looked around the parking lot and seen cars everywhere. The parking lot was packed, and the address just popped in the email twenty minutes ago. He remembered passing a no trespassing sign on his way into the parking lot, so he knew they were on somebody's private property. Whoever they were, they clearly had money. Charlie noticed a few guys in black T-shirts with the word security printed in big white letters on the back of their shirts. They patrolled the parking lot to assure nobodies car got broken into. Least that's what he thought.

"Something is not right about this." Charlie complained. He took the keys out of the ignition and put them in his pocket. Ronnie looked at his older brother. His whole demeanor was tense. He sat in the driver seat with a serious facial expression and with his military haircut. Ronnie couldn't help but grin.

"I brought you here to loosen up."

"I am loose."

"Yeah right. You talkin about something ain't right at a free concert. You know how crazy that sounds?" Charlie smiled. He let out a brief laugh. Ronnie was right. Paranoia was ridiculous. They were there to have a good time and here he was crashing the party before it started.

"I'm sorry." Charlie said. "The military side of me. It's hard to shut off. Let's go on in."

The brothers got out of the car. Charlie looked at the sky. The sun was setting, and the parking lot was filling with anxious teenagers who came to hear the bands play. Like most secret concerts, it had a list of rules. One, was the people would have to show up before the gates locked. The invite warned once the gates are locked, no one could come or go until the concert was over. The brothers walked into the building. The place was a tremendous abandoned factory. It was gutted out and made to use for the concert. It was packed and people bumped into one another. The band called "Evil Genius" readied themselves on the stage as their fans screamed with excitement. Ronnie looked at his watch. The time was 7:30 p.m.

"The concert is about to start." he yelled to his brother Charlie who was standing next to him.

"I hope Karen makes it." Charlie said.

"Don't worry. They still have 30 minutes until the doors lock. This is "Evil Genius" we are talking about. Karen would rather lose a limb then miss this concert." Ronnie said with a smile. "As a matter of fact, here they come now." The boys watched Karen and Anna through the crowd.

"Hi Charlie!" Karen said with a smile.

"Why you so cheesy Karen?" Ronnie teased, already knowing the answer.

"As if you needed to ask." Karen replied, pointing to her black and purple "Evil Genius" t-shirt.

“Okay everybody. The doors are about to lock.” The announcer said over the microphone. “I hope you all are ready for the party of your lives.” he said, walking across the stage. “Ladies and gentlemen, I bring to you, “Evil Genius,”

“Evil Genius! Evil Genius!” The crowd chanted.

The crowd cheered as the band walked onto the stage and played the songs their fans liked. The crowd moved like hypnotic snakes to their tunes. Their music vibrated throughout the building and the full moon rose to its peak. The musicians played loud on their instruments until the moon released their beast like nature. The musicians fell to the stage and began to scream in pain. Their screams turned into grunts. The crowd watched in confusion. Charlie looked to the security. They were experiencing the same thing with the people in the V.I.P. section.

“We have to go.” Charlie said, grabbing Karen by the hand.
The four of them headed towards the entry doors. They pushed on the lever, but the door hardly moved. That’s when they realized the doors had been chained from the outside.

“Damn! The doors are locked.” Charlie said, scanning the area. “There has to be another way out.”

Deep inside, he knew something was wrong from the moment they arrived. He had a bad feeling and the feeling hadn’t left. He knew it wasn't the time to panic. It was the time to take charge. He scanned the area once more and spotted a metal door with the word stairs written on it.

"This way!" Charlie said.

Shoving himself through the crowd, he led them toward the stairwell. Screams began pouring out throughout the crowd. Charlie looked over and seen a huge wolf like creature tearing a girl in half. Other wolf like creatures began attacking people from within the crowd. Some pounced off where the V.I.P. sat. A group of wolves pulled their prey onto the stage and dismembered their victims while they were still alive. Suddenly, it all became clear to Charlie. They had walked into an ambush. They had been doomed from the very start. The sponsors had led them in like sheep to the slaughter.

"God, please? Let the door be unlocked." he said to himself. He grabbed the doorknob and twisted it. The door opened and the four of them rushed in and shut the door behind them. The stairway was small with a flight of stairs that led into two directions. One went up to the next floor and further up to the roof and the other led to the basement. Charlie had no idea what was on the floors above, so he used his military training. Feeling the better tactic would be to barricade themselves in a room or something, he led them to the basement. The basement was wide. Unfortunately, Charlie didn't see any windows. The room had large concrete blocks that kept the room cool. Charlie closed the iron doors and locked it.

"This should buy us some time." he said.

He looked at Karen and she was shaking. Anna, on the other hand, had been crying so hard that she pissed herself.

"What are we going to do now?" Ronnie asked. Charlie could see the confusion and fright in his face.

"We need to barricade that door and find something to use for weapons."

"We are going to die!" Anna screamed! "What the fuck?"

"Shhhhhh!" Ronnie said. He put his finger against her mouth. "Be quiet!" "We don't want them to hear us." he said. Anna pulled away from Ronnie.

"What do you mean be quiet? They are all going to kill us!"

"Calm down! Nobody's going to die Anna. If you follow my instructions, we are all going to get out of here alive." Charlie explained. He looked at both of the girls. "I need you to spread out and find us anything we can use for weapons, and Ronnie, you help me barricade the door."

The brothers looked around the basement but couldn't find anything big enough to put in front of the door. That's when Ronnie found a crowbar. I found something, he said, taking the metal bar to Charlie.

"That will work just fine." Charlie said. He placed a crowbar between the two oval shaped handles on the metal doors.

"This should hold them off." he said, giving the door a hard push to make sure it would hold. To his surprise, the crowbar worked very well. The door hardly moved an inch.

"Come on." he said. "Let's help the girls find something to protect themselves with or perhaps a way out."

The basement was enormous. Charlie estimated it had to be the size of a field. Old printing machines filled the room. Some of the machines still had big rolls of paper attached to them. The scent of flat ink and stale paper dominated the room. The girls had ventured out of sight, so the brothers went out to find them. Blood covered the concert floor and the wolves walked about as the victors. There were very little survivors left and those who were still alive were wishing they were dead because of the pain and loss of limbs. Cries echoed throughout the building as the wolves tore and devoured the flesh of their victims. The announcer walked among the creatures as if he was invisible. As Spike was walking among the carnage, he stepped on something and as he lifted his shoe up, he saw a golden ring with ancient writing on it. From the look of the writings, he surmised it was an enchanted ring. He had no idea what it did, but he had seen one like it before centuries ago. Since he was in the V.I.P. section he figured one of the V.I.P's must have dropped it. He happened to put it on his finger. A perfect fit.

"Release the chains from the door, he ordered on his walkie talkie." The front door opened, and four men stepped in.

"Should we take everyone to the truck and lock them in?" one of the men asked?

"No, some of them are still eating. Start disposing of the bodies for the ones who have finished." The announcer demanded.

He sat on the stage and watched the four men pile the bodies' one on top of another. The smallest man collected the body parts and the announcer smirked. He had hosted many of the raves for Anthon although he was an elder wolf himself, he never participated in the feasting festival, but he did take pleasure in watching his fellow brothers and sisters enjoying themselves. He had once been a ranking member on the world council, but he stepped down because of his change of views. He felt the council had become too sympathetic towards the human race. The council panel changed from witches, vampires, and wolves, to human, witch, vampires, and wolves. Three of each race now made the world council panel. The way Spike seen it, humans weren't worthy enough to rule on a world board because they were the weakest species and a food source. He felt the old ways were better when the humans worshiped them as Gods or tended to them. The wolves were free back then and there were no stipulations and laws pertaining to their activities and food source. Those were the days he thought to himself. Snapping back from his thoughts, he realized his family was finished eating. The wolves went about sniffing and circling the bodies. Without a doubt, they were listening for heart beats, but the announcer knew everyone was dead because too much time had passed. They would have bled out for sure. It was now time to pack up and get ready to go. It wasn't long before the wolves were placed in their cages within a truck and the pile of bodies was placed in a dump truck that would be taken to be disposed of. The announcer looked at his watch and it was 3:00 a.m. He had four hours before the transformation kicked in and the wolves became human again. He stepped back into the building to make sure everything was going as planned. That's when he heard four set of heart beats coming from the basement.

"Someone is here." the announcer said. "You guys get everything ready to go. I'll take care of this."

He began taking of his clothes until he stood there naked. Then he transformed into a huge wolf. In wolf form, his senses were acute. He could smell four distinctive odors and a strong scent of urine. He pursued the trail. It wasn't long before the brothers found Karen and Anna coming out one of the old dusty offices.

"We found a way out." Karen said.

She grabbed Charlie by the hand and then took them into the office. There it was. A big basement window and it was big enough for all of them to get through. The problem was it was blocked by a bunch of heavy wooden crates.

"Help me move these crates." Charley said looking at Ronnie and the girls.

"It's going to take the four of us to move these things."

The girls nodded their heads and grabbed a corner of the crates. One by one they moved the crates until they no longer blocked the window. A hard slam echoed from the basement door. Its metal sounded like thunder with every forceful impact. It wasn't long before the creature knocked down the door and galloped through the basement. It spotted the four. They stood in a room through a doorway. They stared straight at the creature. Fear radiated from the four and the wolf could smell it. It arched its body in a cat like stance. Its long black fur stood up on its body like spikes. Its long sharp teeth oozed with drool. The wolf pounced full force at them only to be blocked by the door frame. Its huge massive body knocked the cement from the walls as it chopped wildly at the teens clawing repeatedly at the wall. The frame and wall began to cave in. A large wooden beam fell down on the wolf's neck rendering it limited movement. The beast struggled under the beam. It swung the back of its body back and forth trying to shake itself free. Charley glanced at the beast for just a moment knowing they had very little time before it got free. Charlie grabbed a push broom from out of the counter. He banged it against the window. It broke the glass.

"There's not much time." he yelled. "Ronnie, you go first."

Ronnie looked at his brother without hesitation. He climbed the crate, grabbed the window seal and pulled himself through. Shattered glass lay outside the window, but Ronnie pushed the pain out of his mind and crawled over it as if it wasn't there. His mind was focused on one thing. Survival! He quickly brushed some glass out of the way with his foot. Then he squatted down and reached into the window.

"Give me your hands." he said.

Anna grabbed his hand and he pulled her through the window. The beast managed to break free. It swung its massive paw at Charley and with one powerful strike; it took his head off of his shoulders. Blood spewed from the open wound and all over Karen. She screamed and wiped the blood from her face with her fingers. The creature grabbed her by the arms and tore her in two. Tears fell from Ronnie's eyes as he witnessed the deaths of Karen and his brother. Paralyzed by fear, he couldn't move. Stuck in a trance like state, he just stared as the wolf chewed on his brother's body like a chew toy.

"Come on Ronnie." Anna pleaded, in a whimper. "We have got to get out of here before they get us. Ronnie, snap out of it."

He knew Anna was right. She mustered up the strength and the two headed to the parking lot. The parking lot was filled with cars, but there was no personal around. The place was quiet except for crickets. Anna and Ronnie jumped the fence and then headed to Anna's car. They stayed crouched down so no one could see them until they finally reached Anna's car. The doors were unlocked so they both got in. Anna nervously reached into her pocket and got her keys. He hand was shaking like crazy. She put her keys in the ignition then turned the keys. The radio came on, but the car didn't start.

"What the fuck!" Anna panicked!

"Stay calm." Ronnie whispered. "I'm sure it's nothing serious. When I get to the hood, pop it quietly." Ronnie said. He slowly got out of the car and headed to the front of the car and lifted the hood.

"Damn!" he said. Crawling over to the driver seat where Anna sat. He opened up her door.

"What is it." Anna asked?

"The guts are ripped out. This car is totaled. We have to find another car."

“Can’t we use your brother’s car?”

“No, he had the keys on him.”

“How are we going to get home?”

“I don’t know Anna. It looks like we have to walk.”

Anna looked at Ronnie with a serous face and said, “I don’t think that’s a good idea, but it’s our only choice.”

“I don’t either. The moon is about to set. I think we should stay put until the sun rises. You get some rest Anna and we will leave at daybreak.”

Ronnie popped the trunk of Anna’s car looking for anything he could use as a weapon. He found a baseball bat, glove, and ball. Anna’s brother must have left it in her trunk after his practice. Ronnie took the metal bat and got back in the car.

“Get some sleep Anna. I got you!”

Anna dozed off for just a second when she was awakened by a loud crash of broken glass. She looked over to the passenger seat where Ronnie was sitting. It was covered with blood and broken glass from its window. Anna panicked and jumped out of her car. She ran fast toward the parking lot entrance. She tripped over something and landed face down in the gravel. She turned her face and seen Ronnie's remains. It was him she had tripped over. She struggled to get on her feet. A wolf pounced on top of her and with one bite, it ripped out her throat.

♀♀♀

DOMON AND DILLION

Chapter Nine

Domon walked into Sterlin Police Department. The place was more secure than he had expected. It had state of the art cameras and a buzz in door. An Officer sat at a desk behind a bullet proof glass.

"How can I help you?" The fat Officer asked still chewing on a jelly donut. Domon showed his badge.

"I'm here to see Captain Dillion. I'm Agent Domon Status."

"One moment sir."

The Officer picked up the phone and dialed an extension. Domon knew he was calling Dillion. A second later the Officer buzzed him through.

"Just follow the trail of desks." the Officer said. "His office is all the way in the back."

Domon walked through the metal door and the place was packed. Officers went about doing their duty like busy ants on a farm. They didn't seem to notice him which was a relief. He headed down the lines of desks until he spotted Dillions office. The door was already opened so he stepped in.

"Nice to meet you Agent Status." the big man said standing from behind his desk. He reached out his hand and shook Domon's hand. "Why don't we sit down and let's get to business." he said. Dillion handed him a folder with the words classified written on it. "For your eyes only!" He instructed. Domon took the folder and looked through it for a moment and Dillion waited for him to finish. "Cecil spoke highly of you." Dillion said. "Hopefully you can wrap this up quickly and things can get back to normal."

"That's the plan." Domon said, placing the envelope on his lap. "Is that all?" he asked, as he was getting ready to leave.

"No, I'll be teaming you up with one of my detectives." Dillion explained. "She's one of our best, sharpest, smartest, and observant. Her Father was also of assistance to the National Council and also a good friend of mine. Right now Detective Spears is under a lot of pressure by Internal Affairs. They think she is a dirty cop."

"Is she dirty?" Domon asked.

"No, she's just loyal, even though her partner is deceased. She still refused to say anything bad about the man. My guess, she didn't want to mess up his family's pension.

"I can respect that."

"Even if I agreed, I could never admit it." Dillion said with a smile.

"I'm sure Cecil told you, I prefer to work alone. A partner would only slow me down."

"It wasn't my call Domon. It was the Council. They feel the mission has to be worked during the day and in the open. The public demands answers and a criminal. It's going to be your job to see both sides get justice."

"So, the hard part is on me?" Domon shrugged.

"It seems that's why Mr. Status." Dillion chuckled.

"Trust me when I say this, she's rough around the edges, but once you get to know her, you'll be glad you had her."

"You realize a lot of these people aren't human which minimizes her chance of living?"

“Miss Spears is sharp and tough. She can hold her own. I’m sure she will be fine.”

“So, what happens when she sees too much and starts to put things together? Cases like this are supposed to be conducted off the record.” Domon explained.

“We will deal with that if it happens.” Domon shook his head.

♀♀

JUSTIN AND THE CARDINAL

Justin arrived at the Cardinals address right on time. After his meeting at the church he spent the rest of the day driving around and sight-seeing. The Cardinal lived in a large white house with a brown picket fence. The yard was well attended to and the porch light was on. He walked to the door and rang the doorbell. The Cardinal answered the door and invited him in. The two walked to the Cardinals study room. It was a room filled with books and two couches.

"Before we get started, would you like a drink or something?"

"No thank you Cardinal. I'm not thirsty."

"You don't need to be so formal here. We are not at the church. Just call me Peter. Anyways, thank you for coming Mr. Ray. I had you meet with me because I'm somewhat familiar with the history of the church events on and off the record. You must understand for the protection of the faith some documents and information are sealed and can only be disclosed to those of the highest order. Are you sure the voice said Blood Moon Dragon?"

"Yes, I'm certain of it. What does it mean?"

"Mr. Ray, I'm going to share with you some secrets of the highest order. Some of it may sound crazy, but I assure you, it's all true. I'm only telling you this because I feel your visions are true and it was by the will of God that I was on that panel today. Had I not have been, the world would be well on its way to experience a hell like no other. I believed I was blessed to learn the secrets in order to help you. In the 14th century, when Rome was at its strongest, and the Catholic faith was flourishing across the world, the Pope, his army, and most of Vatican City was killed in a single night by an inhuman creature who fed on human blood with the ability to transform into a great Dragon. It attacked with fury. The carnage was logged as the worst ever experienced in human history and still in our history up till today."

"Those must've been the images I seen in my vision." Justin pondered.

"I believe they were. The Dragon was the first nonhuman the church had ever encountered, but it wasn't the last. But that is for another story. Fortunately for the church after the Dragon destroyed everything, it left and never came back. This gave the church enough time to rebuild."

"So, you're telling me creatures and Dragons exist?"

"Yes Mr. Ray. Creatures of darkness are among us. However, there is only one Dragon that we know exists. He is the only one that we have any record of. So please, be open-minded and allow me to finish. Upon rebuilding the church, it opened a special unit of unique skilled priests and hunters whose job it was to investigate and hunt these creatures of the night. I don't know if these sectors of the church are still active. If they are, I have no idea where they are. Once the church collected their Intel, they later found out the Dragon's name was Nithael. He was the first vampire, the father of all vampire races. More powerful than the elders, the ancients, the originals, even the Dracula's. He is a direct blood ancestor of Nataasha, the Queen of all Damned. I am sure you are familiar with the self-announced Vampire rock star Leestat?"

"Of course."

"It was later covered up by the church and others to say there was something in the water. Natasha was bad, but the dragon will be pure hell. It is said he is half demon and the first warlock, the only apprentice and blood descendant to Lucifer." Justin looked at the Cardinal. His demeanor was now serious.

"How can we prevent this from happening?" he asked.

"According to your vision Mr. Ray, that is impossible. All we can do is follow the instructions from your vision and pray that will be enough."

"Okay, but tell me how am I supposed to find the priesthood of Yahoel? Even the anthropogenic have concluded they no longer exist."

"You have something they didn't have Mr. Ray. You have God on your side, and an ex-eminence who has had clearance to the secret chambers. He now owns an antique shop in Sterlin City. I'll call him then send you with a note to verify you came for me. He will point you in the right direction. You can stay here for the night. All my books are at your disposal and I'll show you to the guest room."

"Thank you Cardinal."

"Call me Peter."

♀♀♀

ANTHON CELEBRATES

Chapter Ten

Light flickered from the fireplace. It gave the book filled room an orange glow. Anthon sat calmly in his study and across from him was his two business associates, Frank and Spike. A small wooden table separated the three, two on both ends and one in the middle. A silver bucket filled with ice and an expensive bottle of Moet sat on a tray along with three Champagne glasses. Anthon took the bottle and popped the top. He poured the wine into three Champagne glasses, then sat each in front of his friends. He sat the bottle on the table and picked up his glass.

"Too another successful feast." he toasted. The three lifted their glasses and saluted.

"We made over thirty-six million dollars." he said sliding the two fat envelopes across the table. Both men picked up their yellow envelopes. "There's fifty thousand in each. That's your bonus money. So, go out and enjoy yourselves. The real money is being transferred into your accounts as we speak." Anthon said. The two men nodded their heads.

“What’s our next location?” Frank asked. He had hoped Anthon had listened to his advice about shutting down.

“Washington D.C.” Anthon answered. He took a sip of his Champagne then looked at Spike.

“The next feast will be in six months, as always I need you to get things ready.”

Spike nodded. He knew exactly what that meant because he had done it many times before. Find a good location and grease the right palms. So, the right people look the other way. Spike felt anybody he bought, Police, Mayors, Governors, even the Senators, they all had their price and it was his job to find it. Whether it be money, black mail, or even brute force. Spike enjoyed being on the front line. Especially for a cause he believed in. That’s why he took the job of hosting the raves. Frank sat quietly in his seat trying to muster up the strength to announce what was really on his mind.

“I would like to retire!” He blurted out. The two men looked at him like he was crazy.

“What do you mean retire?” Anthon asked! His hospitality face completely diminished.

"I've been doing a lot of thinking." Frank said taking a gulp of his drink. "I feel it's time for me to do something different with my life. Maybe find a good woman and have a few kids."

"We all pledged our lives to the cause Frank." Anthon reminded him.

"I know Anthon, but I've been on your side since the day you took me off the streets and made me the wealthy man I am today and for that I have repaid you with my loyalty and I will continue to do so until my dying day. I just don't feel the way I used too."

Anthon didn't need to ask what Frank meant. He could see the struggle in Frank's face. It had suddenly become clear. Frank no longer had the stomach to do the raves. Frank had now become a weak link who knew everything about their operations and the people in it. Frank picked a hell of a time to have a change of heart especially with the council agent hot on their trail. If Frank was to get caught, there was a chance he would sell him out especially if they promised him immunity or a new life. Anthon couldn't see Frank giving him up, but he knew Frank's mind was made up and there was no changing it. If anyone else would have asked to get out he would have killed them in an instant, but Frank was his best friend and the only person whose loyalty was without question. Not to mention, he was the only person he trusted.

"Who's going to cover your companies' part on the raves?" Anthon asked.

"I have an assistant. He's a wolf like us. I've taught him everything I know. He's as good as me so everything will run smooth."

"Are you sure?" Anthon asked as if he was thinking about it.

"Yes Anthon. I'm positive."

"Okay, set up a meeting with Spike and your assistant and we will take it from there."

"Thank you, Anthon. I knew you would understand." Frank said happily.

"Well, it's time for me to turn in." Anthon announced, while standing up.

He shook both men's hands and walked them to the door. Spike was the first one to walk out the door and once they got halfway to their cars, Anthon called Spike back for just a moment, and Frank got into his car relieved feeling like a huge weight had been lifted off of his chest.

♀♀♀

ANGEL AND DOMON MEET IN DILLION'S OFFICE

Angel walked into Dillions office. She had no idea what he wanted. She was just told to report to him. Once she clocked in, she noticed a man sitting in a chair only a few feet away. He sat there facing the Captain. Even when she entered the room, Domon didn't bother to turn around and see who walked in. She found that odd but disregarded it. Domon sat with his back to Angel. The moment he had dreaded had come upon him. He caught her scent before she entered the room, so he had no need to turn around. He already knew who she was. The lady he had rescued from the park. The only one who could identify him from the sketch. Angel stepped closer and recognized Domon's briefcase. She almost didn't recognize him because of the expensive business suit he wore. It was the luggage tag that gave it away. Caught off guard, her mind raced for her next move. Her first thought was to walk over and arrest him, but then she thought against it. What was Domon doing there sitting in Dillion's office as he had done nothing wrong? Better yet, what had really happened in Sterlin Park? Why was there a headless victim and not a beast? Angel had a lot of questions that needed to be answered, and she felt Domon knew the answers, so she played it cool and heard Dillion out.

"Detective Spears, this is Agent Status." the Captain said. Still seated behind the desk, Domon stood up and shook Angel's hand.

“Nice to meet you.” he said as if that was the first time they met. Domon’s actions were suspicious. Clearly, he knew who Angel was, but she played along with them.

“Nice to meet you too, Agent Status.”

“Agent Status is with the Central intelligence unit.” Dillion explained. He opened the cigar box that sat on the corner of his desk and took out a cigar.

“You guys will be working together on these cases.” Dillion said, reaching in his desk for a lighter. “You both have different sources of Intel and resources. Use them together to get these guys off the streets.” Dillion set his gaze on Angel and lit his cigar. “I know you don’t like partners, Ms. Spears, and I understand why. Especially with your current situation, but I need you to be open with Agent Status.” Dillion said. He took a puff of his cigar and blew out a cloud of smoke. “You two take the rest of the day off and get your thoughts together and get some rest. I need you two sharp and ready first thing in the morning.” Dillion said. The two stood there waiting as if there was something else, they were waiting on Dillion to say. The bald black man looked up at the two.

“That will be all.” he said.

Domon and Angel left Dillion's office and walked to Angel's desk. Domon took a chair from an empty desk next to Angel's and placed it in front of Angel's desk. Angel waited until Domon sat down, then she spoke her mind.

"Look, I'm not sure of what's going on or why you didn't want Dillion to know you saved me, but since were going to be working together and you're going to be using my desk, let me tell you my rules so there is no misunderstanding." Angel took the pictures she had framed off her desk and stuffed them in the bottom drawer of her desk. She placed her coffee mug in there too and a few color highlighters. "You can use my computer desk and all the other drawers, but stay away from my bottom drawer, it's off limits. So, please respect my privacy." Domon looked at Angel and chuckled. Her request had sounded a bit extreme, but he could respect it.

"No problem." he said.

"Your space is your space. Is there anything else I can't touch?"

"Not at the moment, no, but I'll be sure to tell you if something comes up."

Domon stood up, and Angel noticed the folder underneath his arms. She couldn't see the whole word, classified, but she observed the first four letters and concluded that is what it said. She also noticed the folder was much bigger than her own.

"Is that your case file?" She asked. Domon started to lie, but he knew she was smarter than that, so he told the truth.

"Yes, it is. Why don't we compare a few notes before we leave? That way we are getting a head start."

"That sounds good." Domon lied, "but I'm really tired. I can barely keep my eyes open. How about I bring you a copy of the file tomorrow, that way you will have your own and you can make me a copy of yours?"

Angel knew Domon was lying to her. The man looked wired like he'd just finished an energy drink, not to mention he hadn't yawned, not one time. Angel concluded there is something in the folder that Domon didn't want her to see because the copy machine was only a few feet away from her desk, and she knew Domon could see it. Domon had chosen to start their partnership off with a lie instead of telling her the truth. This was a bad move. At first, Angel didn't really know how she felt about Domon, but now she knew for sure she didn't like him.

♀♀♀

FRANK AND DARLA

Chapter Eleven

Frank and Darla were sound asleep in Frank's king size bed when his phone rang. Not wanting to wake Darla from her peaceful slumber, he hurried and grabbed his phone off the nightstand. He didn't even notice the call came up private.

"Hello." he answered.

"You asleep?" Spike asked.

"I'm up now, what's up?"

"I'm sorry to wake you brother, but I need to see you right now."

"Right now?" Frank complained. He looked at the clock on his phone. "Its two o'clock in the morning, can't it wait?"

"I wish it could brother, but it can't."

"Well what's it about?"

"It's about my meeting with your replacement."

"What about him, Frank asked?"

"I would rather run these things by you instead of letting Anton find out." Spike said, as if something was wrong.

"Give me about an hour to get everything together." Frank said, pulling himself up out of bed.

"I'll see you there."

Frank hung up the phone and looked at Darla as she lay naked on the blue satin sheets. Her perfect figure and caramel skin seemed to glisten in the moon light. He loved Darla and everything about her. Not only was she beautiful, she was smart, caring, and loving. It was her sense of empathy toward all living creatures that stole his heart. He vowed to his pack never to have a serious relationship with a human, but Darla had taken his heart by force, and he loved every minute of it. Darla rolled over and looked at him.

"I love you so much." she mumbled, still waking up.

"I love you more." Frank assured her with a heart-felt smile.

Spike was on the expensive business yacht, when he heard gravel from the parking lot. He peeked through the blinds and seen Frank and Darla getting out of Frank's Bentley. He looked at his watch and it had been more than twenty five minutes since his call, clearly, which was not enough time for Frank to drive across town to pick up his secretary Darla and arrive there, which meant Darla had been with Frank earlier when he had called, just as he had hoped. Frank and Darla did a good job at keeping their relationship a secret. Unfortunately for them, everybody makes mistakes and their time was when Spike showed up to talk business unannounced and found Frank and Darla in his office. The room reeked of sex and he could smell it on the both of them. Spike felt some type of way about it. He felt wolves should not sleep outside their species. However, he kept his mouth shut because he felt it didn't interfere with their business, but now Frank had announced he wanted out and Spike knew it was because of Darla. Frank had chosen a human over their race and Anthon was allowing him to do it because of the loyalty he had for their friendship. Spike knew that Anthon had let his emotions cloud his better judgment and Spike understood a move like that could destroy the whole organization because it would appear the leadership showed favoritism among one another. Although, he explained his feelings to Anthon when Anthon called him back in the house that night, Anthon stuck by his decision. Frank is free to go, and no harm is to come to him, Anthon ordered, with a serious face, or they will deal with me. Frank and Darla headed up the dock and Spike went above the deck to meet them.

"Sorry for the inconvenience brother, but this couldn't wait. You guys go below the deck and get comfortable." Spike said. "I'll be right down." Spike then tied the rope from the dock and went up to set the boat on its course, and then he went below deck with Frank and Darla. Frank had already made himself a drink. He stood behind the bar when Spike entered the room. Darla sat on the couch going through paperwork.

"Why don't we take this above deck." Spike said. "There is a beautiful breeze going on."

The three of them went above deck to the patio and sat down. Spike sat across the table from Frank, and Darla sat in the chair next to him. Darla handed Spike a folder.

"Here is everything you asked for, and it's all in alphabetical order." Darla said. Spike took the folder then look at Frank's glass. He was almost out of wine.

"Darla, could you please grab us more wine?" Spike asked nicely. Darla looked over to Frank as to get his consent. Frank gave her a quick nod. A que that meant give them a moment. She took her time going to get the wine. The folder was on the table, so Spike looked at the folder then stopped. "Read the speech here." he said. He slipped the papers across the table. Frank picked up the folder and began to read it.

"What paragraph?" he asked, while looking down at the folder. He didn't even notice Spike's hand reaching under the table.

"Read the whole page." Spike said grabbing the small 380 he had taped under his table. He pointed the small gun at the top of Frank's head and let off two shots. One hit Frank in the head and the other in the chest. Frank didn't see it coming. Darla was down in the bar area when she heard the shots unsure of what she just heard. She ran up the stairs to the upper deck and saw Frank laid out on the floor by the table. Spike was nowhere in sight. Not thinking, she rushed to Frank and held him in her arms. She noticed blood dripping from his head. Suddenly she felt the cold steel barrel of a gun on the back of her head. She heard a bang. She felt a thump, a surge of pain, and then everything went black. Spike turned Frank's body over and shot him once more in the chest. The silver bullet exploded his heart. Spike took Frank and Darla's bodies and threw them overboard. It didn't take long for the sharks to come swarming. Spike took out his phone and called his lieutenant. Nitti answered on the first ring.

"How can I help you boss?"

"I need you to put together a cleanup crew for a car. I'll send you the address. No one can know about this." Spike said, "So use your most trusted guys."

"I got ya boss. Nobody will speak a word." Nitti assured him.

Spike hung up the phone and thought about what Anthon had said. No harm is to come to Frank, or they will have to deal with me. Killing

Frank didn't bother Spike at all. He felt he was doing Anthon a favor. Frank was weak and compromised. This time around humans had made him soft. Frank had lost sight of the big picture and Anthon was letting him walk away. For that reason, Frank got what he had coming. Anthon's order at the house had fallen on death ears. Spike knew how good the organization was running. He had been in many of them during his thousands of years on earth. Spike understood that Anthon's decision would display weakness in the leadership, seeing that every member vowed death before abandonment. The council's assassin couldn't have come at a better time. Frank's disappearance would seem like the assassins work since they wouldn't have a body. The way he seen it he was in the clear. Anthon would never find out, but if he did, the things Anthon would do to him would have him praying for death. Anthon had a thing for torture and he wouldn't be an exception, but he didn't have to worry because he had seen the pool of sharks surrounding the bodies moments after he had thrown them in the ocean and by now, they were shark food. That left him with one problem, the assassin.

♀♀

JACK AND SONYA ON THE MOUNTAINS

Chapter Twelve

The wind blew hard throughout the high Montana Mountains and the rocks felt extremely cold under Jack's fingers. Although he had on the best mountain climbing gear available, it didn't make much of a difference with the subzero temperatures they were encountering from climbing high up in the mountains. They had been climbing over an hour and the weather was awful. The sky was overcast with thick gray clouds which told Jack there is a possibility of a storm coming. Jack looked up at his older sister Sonia who was scaling the mountain with ease. When she looked down at him and noticed he was a ways behind.

"Speed it up!" she said. "We still got to set up camp before the sun goes down." Jack gave his sister a dirty look.

"Not everybody can climb like a monkey." he complained while grabbing the next rock and attempting to catch up.

“Quit your bellyaching!” Sonia laughed. “We’ve climbed harder mountains than this one before.”

“Yeah, that’s easy for you to say!” Jack said, finally catching up to Sonia. Sonia looked over to Jack and smiled. Her long blonde hair braided into a ponytail. It dangled under her pink skullcap and sat on her back.

“According to the map, there should be a ledge a few feet ahead.” Sonia explained. “Once we get there, we’ll find a good place to set up in.”

Jack gave her nod and kept climbing. He was eager to get it over with. His arms were burning, and his fingers were numb. He was a tad bit out of shape. Unlike his sister Sonia, who was healthy, energetic, and had a very athletic body. The ledge wasn’t far at all. They just couldn’t see it because of the clouds in the fog. Jack took off his backpack and set it on the ground. His body was on fire. He had no intention of going on any further. He just wanted to set up the tents.

“Change of plans.” Sonia said. “I found a small opening that leads into a big cave. We will set up there and make a fire. The cave will help keep us warm.”

Jack smiled. Leave it to his sister to find a cave in below zero weather. Sonia was right. A cave would be much warmer than a tent out in the open.

“Are you sure no bears are in there?” Jack asked.

“Don’t be silly little brother. This isn’t bear country and I’ve already checked for mountain lions. The cave is safe.”

The two climbed in the hole and began to unpack. The sun was still up so it provided enough light to see. Jack took the tent out of his bag along with the canned goods and eating utensils. He looked at Sonia. She was working on setting the fire.

“I need to get this fire going.” She said, “Or it’s going to be dark and extremely cold.” Jack looked up at Sonia. Her fingers were beet red. Almost too cold to move but she did a good job of hiding it.

“Put your hands between your thighs for a moment. Use your body heat to warm your fingers, and then try.” Jack suggested.

Sonia took a timeout to warm her hands and watched Jack put up the tents. She was surprised to see that Jack had not lost his touch. He had both tents set up in no time. Jack laid Sonia’s sleeping bag in her tent and Sonia gave the fire starting another try. The fire ignited. It lit the cave like a large lamp revealing the now visible writing on the cave walls.

"Look at that!" Jack said, walking over to the wall. Sonya walked over and stood beside Jack.

"Look at all those different writings." she said, "They look like different languages."

"You're right. Some of the writings go back thousands of years and some of it before Christ and others after his death." Jack explained. He stepped closer to get a better look and Sonja smiled.

"There goes the anthropogenic in you." Sonja teased.

"You have no idea what we may have stumbled upon. We may be the first to have entered this cave in over a thousand years."

That couldn't be!" Sonia said. "This place wasn't even that hard to find. Just like I found it in no time, I'm sure others could have also."

"Not if the opening just revealed itself because of the climate. The entrance could have been a block of ice. All of this time and we were just lucky enough to be the first to find it once it melted."
Sonia looked at Jack. She could tell that he was serious about what he was saying, and it did sound logical.

"So, you're saying we are the first people to find this place? Are these drawings or writings worth anything?"

"It's still too early to say, but usually caves like this contain artifacts that may be worth lots of money. Hopefully this is one of those places." Jack walked over to his backpack and took out a pencil and a notebook. "I'm going to have to look around and see what I can translate."

He walked over to look at the writings. Sonia looked at him and smiled. He was still the little explorer he used to be. It didn't matter how many expensive business suits he was dressed in or the lawyer talk that he spoke in the courtroom because Sonia knew he was born to explore. Jack had given up on his job of being an anthropologist because it required him to be out of the country a lot. Although he had no problem with it because he was doing what he loved, his girlfriend of two years felt it didn't pay enough. She convinced Jack to give up exploring and become a lawyer in order to provide for her expensive living habits. A year later, she left him for a wealthy doctor. Jack was devastated. He took time off his job and secluded himself at home to drink these problems away. It took Sonia three months to pull Jack out of that dark place and back into traveling and enjoying life. Sonia reached in her bag and pulled out a big metal pot. She opened the canned goods that Jack had taken out and poured them in the pot.

"Take your time! I'll get dinner ready."

Sonia stirred the stew and Jack adventured off into another part of the cave. Sonia looked up and noticed Jack was gone. "Jack?" She called out to him.

"What's up?"

"You're breaking my concentration."

"Quit complaining. I just wanted to know if you found anything interesting yet."

"As matter of fact I did!" Jack said in a confident tone. "Come here. I'll show you."

Sonia gave the stew one more good stir to make sure it wouldn't burn then covered it and set the pot to the side then went to see what Jack was talking about. Jack stood with a lit torch in his hand, studying the walls.

"Where did you get that torch?" Sonia asked.

"I found it on the floor" Jack replied.

He never took his gaze from the wall. Sonia gave Jack a minute. Clearly, something had caught his concentration. She glanced around the cave seeing it in the light for the first time. The place was big with different chambers. It had torch holders with a couple of torches.

“What is this place?” Sonia asked, fascinated.

“I am not sure.” Jack said. I’ve never seen anything like this before.

If I’m translating this Templar right, this is some kind of secret safe house. The writing hints about it holding something of great importance. You see this eight-pointed cross? It represents the Templar and some secret order that dates back to the early Hebrews before Christ. I think this language is the forgotten language of YAH. This would take a lot of time to research to translate. However, I think the Templar translation is the same message.” Jack said, handing Sonja the torch. “Here, hold this.” he said. He walked over to a big boulder surrounded by a pile of little rocks. He picked up the boulder and set it on the floor next to one of the walls of the cave and he took the torch and placed it next to a torch holder on the same wall. The cave started to shake, and the wall began to rise at the end of the cave. Sonia looked at Jack in amazement. The whole situation was intoxicating. Now she understood the feeling that Jack got every time he found a new discovery. Jack looked at Sonia with a big smile.

“Let’s have a look.” he said.

They walked up to the door and saw that the room was pitch black. Jack took out the small flashlight he had clipped on his belt and the two walked in the light. It wasn’t much. It covered only a small amount of area. It was hard for them to make out the room but then

Jack saw another torch on the wall. He took a lighter out of his pocket and lit the torch. The flame shined bright and illuminated the whole entire room. The place looked like an old armory. Cobwebs covered the rest the armor, swords, spears, and shields. A bookshelf rested against the wall filled with old dusty books. A long wooden table sat in the middle the room with a bunch of chairs around it. Sonia walked to the dust covered table. She could still make out the symbol on it. The symbol was a giant cross.

"Look at all this history!" Jack said.
He went to the bookshelf and pulled a book out and read a passage, then closed the book. "These are not ordinary books." he said. "These are journals going back thousands of years. Think of all the history and secrets contained in all these books."

"Are they worth any money?" Sonia asked.

"Yeah, but to be honest, I'd love to keep them all to myself at least until I read them."

"Stop being so selfish!"

Sonia looked at the books. There were hundreds of them piled on the shelves and neatly stacked on the floor. She looked at the top shelf and noticed a blue cross painted on the wall. She walked over to the bookshelf and noticed it wasn't pushed to the wall. She peeked in between the opening.

“I think there is something behind here!” she said, pushing the wooden bookshelf from the side. The bookshelf easily slid over and revealed a hidden doorway.

“Nice find!” Jack said, impressed, he grabbed the torch out of the torch holder.

“We are going to need some more light.” he said, and the two entered the doorway.

Jack appeared in the doorway. It led down a hall. Nothing looked dangerous as far as he could see; however, he knew to be cautious, because tombs and other sacred places were known to have traps.

“Stay close to me.” Jack said. “This place could have traps.”

Sonia gave her brother a big nod and they headed down the hallway. The pathway took them deep in the mountain’s cave and Sonia was starting to have second thoughts. The fact there could be traps had still worried her.

“Maybe we should go.” she said.

“We’ve come too far.” Jack said.

“Let’s just see what’s ahead, then will go back.”

The two walked about half a mile and finally came to a big wooden door. It looked like it belonged in a tower of some huge castle. Jack tried to open the door and to his surprise it was unlocked. He pushed the door open. He seen a long gold object laid out on a cement slab. The slab was about four feet off the ground and sat in the middle of the room.

"What is it?" Sonia asked not sure what they were looking at or what to think.

"It looks like some kind of tomb." Jack said.

"I'm going to get a closer look."

Jack walked across the room and stood over the object. He studied it for a moment, and then blew some dust off the inscriptions to get a better look.

"That's odd." he said. "These inscriptions look Hebrew, but the sarcophagus looks Egyptian." I've never heard or seen anything like this before. This must be the thing of importance that the writing was hinting about. I believe it's over 2000 years old, dating back to the forgotten language of YAH. I believe this is one of their tombs, but nobody has seen one or found one until now."

"So, this is a new discovery?" Sonia asked. She walked over and stood next to Jack. "This must be worth a great deal of money."

"It is." Jack said. "Technically, we are already rich from this day forth. We will be able to buy what we want. Let's have a look inside."
Jack put the torch in a torch holder then him and Sonia pushed open the sarcophagus and saw a mummy inside. Its hands were tied with a rope and reinforced by a chain.

"You think they buried it alive?"

"It looks that way." Jack said.
He looked at the rope. There is a writing painted on the rope, he said.

"Can you translate it?" Sonia asked.

"We will see in a moment." Jack untied the mummy's hands and looked at the rope closely. "By the authority of Yahoel and the power of Zazriel and the Heavenly Angels we bind thee. It's some kind of binding spell." Jack said. He went to untie the chain. "Fuck!" He yelled snatching his hand back. "I cut myself on that chain."
Jacks hand was covered in blood. He knew he had gotten some on the mummy. Sonia looked at the gash on his hand, and then shook her head. Sometimes he could be a bit clumsy.

"That cut looks deep." she said, taking the flashlight back from Jack. "Stay here while I find a first aid kit."

Before Jack responded, Sonia shot down the hallway. Jack waited by the door and peered down the hall. Suddenly, he heard the sound of chains rattling. He turned around and the torch went out. The room was dark. He heard footsteps coming in his direction. His eyes struggled to adjust. Finally, he could make out the figure standing in front of him right before it tore out his throat. Sonja ran as fast as she could to the front and back. She entered the room and wondered why it was so dark.

"Jack?" she called, but he could not answer. She was headed for the torch when she found Jack's body laid out on the ground. He looked toward the ceiling and blood squirted from his open wound, he moved his mouth, but nothing came out. Jack was trying to tell her something, she just didn't know what. She looked at his finger and realized he was pointing up. She raised her head to look at the creature hanging on the ceiling. It dropped down from the ceiling and pinned her to the ground and buried its teeth deep into her neck. It fed on her until she had no life left.

♀♀♀

ANGEL AND DOMON

Chapter Thirteen

Angel arrived at the station earlier than usual because she couldn't sleep. She spent most of the night tossing and turning. She couldn't stop thinking about Domon and the events that happened in Sterlin Park. There was no doubt she shot a creature, yet they found a man in its place. A man that may have her bullets in him and that most likely will cost her job. Angel shook her head. She was beginning to feel like a character in an episode of the twilight zone. Realizing she had found herself in the middle of something much bigger. Perhaps something she wasn't supposed to know about. She was sure Domon knew what was going on, but almost certainly he wouldn't tell her the truth if she asked him flat out. She knew she would have to be more strategic with the way she pursued the answers. Angel walked to the big metal door and showed her ID to the officer behind the bulletproof glass. The Officer gave her a polite smile and buzzed her in. She looked down the line of her desk and seen Domon sitting at her desk. He didn't bother to sit behind her desk. Instead, he sat in a chair in front of it. He seemed to be studying a case. Apparently, he had started without her. He didn't seem to notice Angel approaching his direction. At least that was what Angel thought. Angel walked up and looked at her desk. There was a big brown folder laying on it.

“It’s your copy of our packet.” Domon said. “Everything the FBI has on your case and others like it.” Domon didn’t bother to look up from the case he was studying nor say good morning and Angel found that unprofessional and a bit rude. She sat at her desk and then fixed her gaze on Domon. He quickly felt her stare. So, he looked up and gave her his attention.

“First off, thank you for saving my life.” Angel said, “But before we go on any further, I think we need to establish an understanding. I’ve come to the conclusion that something is going on. Perhaps something above my clearance, however, I don’t like being in the dark.” Angel said. She studied Domon’s demeanor, but there was no change in his expression and his posture remained the same. Angel continued. “In order for this partnership to work, we have to be open and honest about everything in this investigation. I’ve seen a lot of strange shit that defies the logic of what I believe in. Trust me, I understand the importance of confidentiality and how to keep my mouth shut, but I need to know what I’m up against. I put some of the puzzle together, but since I ‘am a no bull shit type of person, I ’am giving it to you straight and I hope you do not insult my intelligence.” Domon sat there for a moment as if he was trying to figure out what to say, then he spoke.

“Captain Dillion said you’re trustworthy and a great detective and I respect his decision, therefore I would not insult your intelligence by lying. Like you said it’s better to be open and honest with each other and that won't be a problem." Domon said. "I've given you copies of everything in my packet except for a couple of documents. I need the proper clearance to show you."

"And when you have the proper clearance?" Angel asked, "That Intel could be valuable information needed to catch our killer." Angel explained, knowing her complaint may be falling on deaf ears.

"I fully understand your grievance Miss. Spears, but you know we all have protocols and procedures we must follow. Let's just focus on what we got right now, and I give you my word, I'll get you that clearance."

Angel didn't like Domon's answers at all. She could tell he was telling her what he needed in order for them to move forward with the case and avoid an argument. Angel picked up the packet and opened it. She was curious to see what was inside. To her surprise, it contained Intel she had never seen before. It had names, pictures, addresses, bank statements, emails, and email passwords of government officials and businessmen along with missing persons' reports and animal attacks.

"What is all this?" Angel asked, looking at the documents more closely.

"It's a glimpse behind the curtain." Domon said. "The perp you're looking for is part of something much bigger. Domon continued to study his folder, giving Angel enough time to skim through the Intel so they could put together a strategy, although Domon already had an overall plan which was to use Angel as a means to lure Anton and his crew out. Domon knew once Angel started poking around their companies and inquiring about the legal business, Anton would be forced to do something about it, and when he did, Domon would be right there waiting and work his way up to the top.

"I had no idea you guys had so much information. I guess it's true. Uncle Sam knows everything. Is this the Fortune 500 Anton Parker?" Angel asked?

"Yes, it is." Domon answered. "We have reason to believe he is a part of a sex trafficking ring that involves extortion, murder, kidnapping, and the list goes on. As you know, Anton is a very successful businessman whose money makes it hard to prosecute any case against him. He has a lot of people on his payroll, which include Judges, Prosecutors, Senators, Officers, etc..."

"So, what does all this have to do with our current case?"

"I believe the killing and the rapes were done by the same two men I've been investigating." Domon explained. "Both men are part of Anton's crew. You will see similar cases in your packet. All the crimes happened in different states all around or during the same time a secret party or concert was going on and those who were said to attend were never seen again."

"So, we have to catch both of Anton's men and possibly prevent a massive kidnapping."

"That seems to be the plan, except we have one killer left. Judging by the man who was killed in the park's tattoos. We believe him to be Carlos Ramsey. He was one of the two men we were looking for."

"Do we have a name on the other guy?"

"No, all we know is that they call him Spike." Angel smiled at Domon. She knew he was still holding back, but she could tell he had made somewhat of an attempt not to lie, so she cut him some slack. She understood trust had to be earned, and not easily given. Perhaps Domon thought the same way. She looked at the clock on the wall. It was 6:30am.

"I never start work on an empty stomach." She said. "Let's get something to eat and then we can get started on the case."

"Sounds good to me." Domon said.

♀♀♀

TIME TO FEAST

The mummy who was once known as Nithael, the Bloodmoon Dragon, walked out of the cave. His bandages covered with the climbers' blood. He looked up at the star filled sky and inhaled the cold mountain air. The sky was beautiful. It had been far too long since he had seen it. In fact, it had been millenniums, but he didn't know it. He thought back to the night he was defeated by the Angel named Zazriel and imprisoned in a sarcophagus by the Holy Monk of Yahoel. It was the binding spell inscribed on the rope that held him prisoner, but now he was free. With a whole new world to explore, he felt a pain in his gut, a clear indicator that he needed more blood. His body was extremely weak. The two climbers had been more like an appetizer than a nourishing meal. It had been far too long since he last fed. His insides were dry and like leather. He needed a lot more life force to gain his full strength and heal his body completely. He wondered what happened to the Angel Zazriel. He was in no shape to fight the Angel again. The wound from the Angel's sword at his side burned and was healing slowly. The sword was one of the only weapons that caused him critical damage. He wondered why Lucifer didn't rescue him from his prison. Surely, he had enough time to find him. He'd summon his old friend later once he gathered his strength. He walked to the cliff of the mountain and looked down. He was too high up to see the bottom. He stepped off the cliff and was falling fast and suddenly transformed into a huge red dragon and took flight across the night sky, his long wings gliding through the air. The wind felt good against his wings. A feeling he wanted to enjoy for a while longer, but time was against him. He had very little energy and he needed to feed before his energy depleted. It didn't take long for him to reach the ocean and he quickly spotted a cargo ship. In his Dragon form, he was able to see heat signatures and he counted about a hundred and ten crew members, which was more than enough to get his fill. He landed on some of the ship's freights. A crew man was passing by. He didn't see the scorpion like tail as it pierced through his back and out of his chest. The tail lifted the Sailor to the top of the crate and Nithael tore a plug of his throat. Twenty minutes later, the whole crew was dead.

♀♀♀

DARLA IN THE HOSPITAL

Chapter Fourteen

Beep! Beep! Beep! The annoying sound beeped in Miss. Doe's ear like a broken smoke detector. She opened her eyes and realized she was in a hospital. The annoying sound had been her heart monitor. She had no idea how she had gotten there, but the sharp pain in her shoulder assured her something had happened. She tried to remember what happened but was met with an excruciating head pain. Her vision was blurry so she waited a moment in hopes that it would clear up. She closed her eyes then counted to ten, then opened them and her vision was much better. She sat up in the bed and then looked around. Another patient lay in the bed across from her. He had his bed positioned up almost like a chair and he was watching Jerry Springer. He was too caught up in his show to notice she had awakened. She looked over to the window. The blinds had been left open perhaps to provide the room with a little bit of sunlight which it did. There were no flowers or balloons at the front of her bed. She wondered why no one had come to support or check on her. Surely, they knew where she was. A nurse entered the room.

"Good afternoon." She said, "I'm glad you're awake."

She picked up a clipboard from the front of Miss. Doe's bed then studied it for a moment.

"How long have I been asleep?" Jane asked.

"About three days."

Miss. Doe couldn't believe the nurses answers. She sat there in silence while the middle-aged nurse looked over her chart. She wrote something down in it then placed it back on the bed.

"How are you feeling?" The nurse asked.

"Ok, I guess. She took her stethoscope and placed it on Miss. Doe's chest.

"Take a deep breath." she said. Miss. Doe took a deep breath then slowly breathed out.

"Your lungs sound clear of any water." The nurse said.

"What do you mean?"

"I'm sorry Miss. Doe. You must have a lot of questions. Can you remember anything that happened?"

"No, and when I try to recall what happened I get a severe headache. I can't remember anything, not even my name."

"That happens a lot with head injuries." the nurse said. "Your memory will come back. Just give it some time. I'm sure you will have your full memory before you know it." She gave Miss. Doe a polite smile and Miss. Doe struggled to give her one back.

"How did I get here?" Miss Doe asked.

"Dr. Kent and his wife brought you in."

"He and his wife were on their yacht when they found you floating in the water. Mr. Kent tended to your wounds and brought you here to St. Matthew hospital. You're lucky to be alive. The slightest bump to your head could have killed you. That's why we got that cushy headband around your head. You are to remain on bed rest until we can get that bullet out of your head."

"And that will be?"

"That depends entirely on Dr. Kent, but I'm sure it won't be long now that you are awake. If you need anything, please hit that little red button next to your bed."

"A small Asian man walked into the room. Hi, I'm Dr. Kent. I'm glad to see you're finally awake. You never know what to expect with a head injury until your patient awakes. You're up looking functional; however, you're not out of the woods yet. As you know you were shot in the shoulder and the head. The bullet went straight through with your shoulder, but your head is a different story. Lucky you have a hardhead. The bullet entered your skull but was stopped before it hit the cerebral part of your brain. If you were to bump your head the wrong way, it would push the bullet through and kill you. Now that you are awake, I'll put you in for surgery tomorrow, so I need you to rest."

"Thank you, Dr. Kent for everything."

"No problem, I'll see you tomorrow."

The Doctor left the room and Miss. Doe picked up the phone on the nightstand next to her bed. She dialed the first number that came to mind in hopes of reaching someone she knew. The phone rang four times until the voicemail clicked on.

"This is Frank, leave a message and I'll get back to you."

The voice on the voicemail, made her heart skip a beat. She knew the person on the voicemail much deeper than a friend. Somehow, she just knew.

"Hi, I'm not sure if we know each other. I'm down at St. Matthew hospital. If I sound familiar, please get in touch with me. Thank you."

A few minutes later, Frank's maid checked the answering machine.

ANTHON AND SPIKE

Chapter Fifteen

Spike pulled up to the tall red security fence on Anton's mansion and watched as two armed guards walked to the fence and left through. One of the guards recognized him and signaled the other guard in the booth to roll the gate. Spike nodded at the guards then headed down the long dirt runway. He never understood why Anthon chose to live in extremely large mansions with acres of land, especially when Anthon chose to live by himself, apart from his help. Spike drove up the long black road and parked by a huge white-water fountain by a giant statue of an Angel. One of Anthon's servants stood at the door to meet him.

"Good afternoon Mr. Solomon."

"Call me Spike, he corrected him.

"My apologies Mr. Spike. Please follow me."

Spike followed the Butler down the long hall and into a door ducked off to the left and there he saw Anthon seated at a table. He had a half full glass in his hand and a bottle of vodka set on the table in front of him. He gave Spike a forceful smile. Spike could tell he was drunk.

"Have a seat." Anthon instructed.
Spike walked over and sat at the table.

"How are you holding up brother?" Spike asked but he already knew the answer.

"I'm good." Anthon answered.

"What's the word on Frank?"

"We still haven't heard from him. He hasn't been to work or home in three days. He hasn't checked his voicemails either. His mailbox is full."

"Have you checked with Darla?" Anthon asked.

"Yes, so far it's the same thing with her. Do you suppose they ran off together?"

"I already gave Frank my blessing. There is no need for him to run off. He would have stuck around to make sure everything was running right with the raves. Even then he would let me know where he is going."

"Who is running Frank's company?"

"His assistant, Mr. Rolan."

"So far, everything is running good, like Frank said. Although we are hoping for the best, I feel it's safe to conclude Frank may have been killed by the Council's agent."

"Fuck! Anthon yelled.

He slung his glass at the wall. The small glass exploded on impact. A small maid quietly came into the room and began cleaning up the glass. Anthon didn't say a word. He waited for the maid to leave the room and whispered to Spike.

"I want him dead! Use all our resources to find the assassin and bring him to me alive. I want to be the last person he sees before I end his life."

"Say no more boss. It will be done."

Spike stood up and headed to his car. He knew that Anthon had nothing more to say. He pulled out of Anthon's driveway and smiled wickedly. Everything had gone exactly like he had planned. He slipped in his Rick Ross CD and turned the music of high. "I'll Ride For My Niggas Dog", the music banged through his 15's and made the whole car rattle. He was now in the clear, but if Anthon had ever found out, the things Anthon would do to him would have him begging for his death. He passed by the deli and cruised through the town. He had no particular place to go. He thought about going to the pub and maybe having a couple of drinks to celebrate, but then his phone rang.

“What’s up Nitti?”

“Boss, we have a problem. Darla is alive!”

♀♀

THE DRAGON LOOKS FOR LUCIFER

Chapter Sixteen

There were more than enough sailors for Nithael to gain his full strength. He just killed everyone on the boat for sheer sport. He sensed a kindred spirit a long distance away. The feeling was faint which meant his ancestor was nearly out of his range of sensing them. He wondered if they could feel him but then he really didn't care. He took the severed arm of a sailor and drew a pentacle on the deck floor. He recited his invocation to summon Lucifer. His words echoed threw out the ship and the boat began to shake. Suddenly Beelzebub, the prince of demons appeared.

"Long time no see my Lord!" The Demon said with a smile. Nithael didn't return the smile.

"Where is Lucifer?" He said. "I want to speak with him."

"Oh, you haven't heard?" "Lucifer was defeated and imprisoned when we went to war with heaven. Satan is the prince of hell now."

“Satan didn’t send a rescue party?” Nithael asked.

“You know how it is with power. Let’s just say it hasn’t been on his top to do list.”

“That’s why he sent you to answer my summons? He didn’t want to face me and displease me with his troublesome news?”

“Perhaps, my Lord! I can’t say what his intentions were, but know this, me and my legion are at your disposal.” The demon said.

“Good, do you know which prison Lucifer is being held in?”

“No, sir, he is in a secret prison. No one knows where he is. It could be somewhere in heaven or earth, but we believe its earth. We also have come up with some more information. Sources say that there are three artifacts, a compass, map, and key. With these items, you will be able to get the location to free Lucifer.”

“Hmmm.” The Dragon thought for a moment, and then he looked at his subordinate. “Send your demons out to get me the location of the artifacts.

“We’ll sir, we already know where the compass is, the General said. My underlings overheard two priests talking about it. Apparently, it’s being kept in an antique shop by a Cardinal who owns the place. The name of the shop is called “Exquisite Goods.” It’s not too far from where you are. It's in Sterlin City. You can use the compass to track the other two artifacts then you will be able to free Lucifer and once again reign over the earth."

"Well then, I better get on my way. Keep me informed Beelzebub."

"As you wish sir."

The demon turned into a puff of black smoke then entered the symbol. Nithael stood there for a moment to organize his thoughts. He wanted to free Lucifer as soon as possible but he had forgotten his most powerful spells. He needed to go over the lexicube (Lucifer spell book) which he had left in a hidden lair in Asia right before he fought the Angel Zazriel. The sun had come up, so he decided to wait until night fall and use the stars as his compass.

♀♀

DARLA IN THE HOSPITAL

Chapter Seventeen

Spike couldn't believe what he was hearing. A flood of thoughts raced to his head. He pulled the car over so he wouldn't crash. He had to get his composure and make sure he heard Nitti correctly.

"Did you just say that Darla is alive?"

"Yeah, I know it's hard to believe, but I checked the facts myself. It's true. Darla is at St. Matthew hospital. She called Frank's house early this morning and left a message on Frank's answering machine and Frank's maid recognized her voice."

"Does Anthon know?"

"He found out today by Frank's maid Rita. She called and told him as soon as Darla left the message.

"Damn, that's a problem!" Spike stressed.

"Yeah, Anthon is getting ready to go up there as we speak, and he also had her moved to her own personal room and he sent some of his personal security to watch over her. So now it's nearly impossible to handle."

"Has she said anything?

"Not yet Boss. Doctors say she has amnesia, but her memory can come back any time."

"If it happens were both dead." Spike complained.

"I know! What do you suggest we do?"

"There is no where we can run that Anthon's money can't find us."

"You're sure none of your men know about the Frank situation?"

"I'm positive. I did the cleanup myself."

"We may have only one choice to assure safety and may be hard to do, both once you do this you will have to leave town until things blow over."

"What is it?"

"We kill Anthon."

♀♀

TIME TO EAT

Chapter Eighteen

Angel took Domon to a small diner not far from the precinct. It was like a three-minute drive. They pulled into the parking lot and Angel cut the engine off.

"Let's get some grub." she said, while getting out the car and closing the door behind her. She didn't give Domon a chance to respond, she was all-ready heading into the restaurant.

She's very energetic, Domon thought to himself getting out the car to join her. They walked into the diner and sat at the table next to the big picture window, with the words "Debbie's Diner" in large yellow letters. Domon looked out the window. The parking lot was empty except for the blue Crown Victoria they had come in. The sun had started to rise, beaming its light over the restaurant into the parking lot. Domon watched as it illuminated the place. A waiter came to their table.

"Good morning! Can I take your orders?"

"I'll have my usual." Angel said, looking across the table at Domon.

She noticed he didn't even bother to read the menu.

"I'd like a coffee black please." said Domon.
The waiter wrote down their orders then said, "Okay, that's one coffee black, one biscuit, and gravy with a side order of bacon and hash browns coming right up." The waiter left to get the orders.

Then Domon asked Angel, "At the precinct, you said that you put together some of the puzzle. What is it that you've come up with?" Angel gave Domon a wicked smile. She knew he was testing her detective skills.

"Judging by the amount of effort it took to secure your cover as a lawyer, and yes I checked it out there were no loopholes with your identity. Now you show up at the station as an FBI agent. Which means, whoever you work for, has a great deal of money and a lot of authority? I'm guessing your NSA, judging from the incident at Sterling Park. The one you never mentioned to Dillion. I'm guessing you are part of that special unit. The one that is only rumored to exist but has never been confirmed. What were they called? Something ...agents."

"Council Agents." Domon finished her sentence for her. "So, you got all of that from our previous run in huh?" Domon asked?

"Am I right?" Angel asked, her smirk turning into a smile.

“Let’s just say, I am not going to confirm or deny anything.”

Angel set her case file on the table.

“There is a lot of information here and we don’t have time to go through it all right now. Since you already have been through it, I’ll follow your lead today and tomorrow. After I finish going over everything, we can put together a strategy.”

“Sounds good to me.” Domon agreed. He opened his case folder. “Turn to page thirty-six and you will see that Willcons Incorporated is under the same LLC Corporation as Anthon Parker. We believe Anthon is using this company to send out the location and invitations for the concerts.

“So, we need a search warrant to check all the companies’ computers, servers, and hard drives.” Angel replied.

“That’s correct, but no Judge is going to give us a search warrant, not without probable cause.” Domon explained.

“Let me guess? Your plan is to shake the place up a bit and maybe they will panic and make a mistake.”

“People tend to make the wrong moves from being paranoid.” Domon explained. Angel nodded in agreement. She liked the way Domon thought. She would have done the same thing. The waiter brought Angel's food and Domon's cup of coffee. The waiter arrived with their orders. Angel wasted no time crushing the biscuit into her gravy. She was starving. She had not eaten since yesterday afternoon nor did it dawn on her to eat anything while she tossed and turned throughout the night. Domon sipped on his coffee and watched Angel finish her breakfast. He wouldn't have to feed for another week. One wolf heart could sustain him for about three weeks and Mark's heart had him energetic. It didn't take long for Angel to finish her breakfast. She left the payment on the table along with a heavy tip. She looked at Domon who had already finished his cup of coffee. She stood up and pushed the chair in behind her. "Time to go to work." she said.

♀♀

DARLA IN THE HOSPITAL

It had been a busy morning for Darla. She loved her new private room. Someone spent a great deal of money making sure she was comfortable. The room was big and comfy, not small and compact like the room she had just left. The room had a lot more luxury. A microwave sat on the counter and a small refrigerator was in the corner of the room. The place gave her a sense of privacy. She didn't have to worry about a breast slipping out or a roommate looking at her but. She looked at the table. It was covered with flowers and balloons, and a big teddy bear sat in a chair next to the table with the words, "Get well soon" on its T-shirt. All was the works of a friend she couldn't remember by the name Anthon Parker. She briefly felt guilty. Not being able to remember who he was, but she appreciated everything he had done. She didn't care much for the security and they seemed to notice, so they stayed out of her way and continued to be posted outside her door. Rita, Frank's maid, had arrived earlier that morning. She was at the hospital at 7:00am on the dot. She brought Darla a duffel bag with clothes, perfume, and feminine products. She also brought Darla's purse, which she found on Frank's dresser. It contained her ID, money, and credit cards. She set her purse on the small stand next to the bed on top of a notepad she had been sketching on. Darla had a craving for pizza so she asked Rita to pick up one along with some cold cuts and other food items she could refrigerate. Darla hated the fact that the doctor wanted her to stay in bed. She had been sitting in it for hours. Sitting up didn't make much of a difference. She wanted to stretch her legs and walk a little. She grabbed the remote control and flipped through the channels. There was a lot to choose from. She turned to the preview guide to look at the time. It was noon, and her stomach was growling. She was wondering what was taking Rita so long. She had been gone for over an hour, but then she caught wind of her own scent. She took a sniff under her arm. She smelled horrible. Disregarding the Doctor's orders, she grabbed a bottle of scented soap and a sponge from her duffel bag and headed to the shower. The water felt so good on her body and she felt she could stand there forever. Unfortunately, she had to be quick or someone might get caught by the nurse. She took the soap and lathered her body good and quickly rinsed herself off. The bathroom was already furnished with clean towels, so she grabbed a towel and exited the bathroom. Tom and Jerry played on the TV. She looked at the dog Spike then it hit her hard.

"The guy that shot me. His name was Spike."

She worried that she might forget the name. She rushed to the nightstand to write it down. She didn't see the duffel bags under her bed. The strap caught her foot like a noose and tripped her as she reached for the bed. Her fingers barely grazed the railing. She hit the floor hard and smacked the side of her head. Everything got fuzzy. A moment later, two nurses ran in.

♀♀♀

WILCON'S INDUSTRIES

Chapter Ninteen

Willcon's Industries was a big building downtown in the heart of Sterlin City. By its architectural structure, Domon could tell it had been around for a long time. Perhaps it was a historical landmark. You'd have to check it out one day. The two walked into the building with its marble floors and state-of-the-art surveillance. The place was busy with people who were coming and going like ants moving about. Angel gave the room a quick scan. There were an excess number of cameras. Angel found that unusual. A guard stood behind a u-shaped counter, while two more guards worked the x-ray machine and metal detector. The two walked over to the counter.

"Welcome to Willcons Incorporated." A guard said. "How can I help you?" Angel flashed her badge.

"I'm Detective Spears and this is Mr. Status. We would like to have a word with Mr. Willcons."

"I'm sorry, Mr. Willcon's isn't here right now. Is there something I can help you with?" Angel shook her head no.

"We need to speak with whoever is in charge."

"That would be Mr. Rolin." the guard said. "Hold on, and I will get him for you." He picked up the phone and dialed an extension.

"There are two detectives down here who need to speak with you."

"I'll be right down."

Domon heard him through the phone. A few seconds later, a young African American man exited the elevator. He walked over to the two.

"Hello! I'm Eric Roland. How can I help you?"

"I'm Detective Spears," Angel showed her badge "and the gentleman with me is one of our company programmers. We have reason to believe your company is involved in some illegal activity. We would like to have a look at your computers, servers, and hard drives."

"Do you have a warrant?" Rolland asked.

"You got something to hide?" Angel replied.

"No maam. It's just procedure. We have a lot of new projects and can't afford the competition to get a hold of our tech. There is absolutely no way I can give you access to our computers or servers without a warrant."

"Okay, I understand." Angel said. "We will be back shortly with your warrant. So please don't go too far."

"I won't Detective. I'll be here all day."

Angel looked at Domon "Let's go to get that warrant."

The two headed towards the exit sign, and then Angel stopped.

"Oh, one more thing, Angel walked up to Roland and handed him her card. Have Mr. Willcons call me."

Roland took the card and put it in his pocket.

"I'll be sure to have him do that."

Roland watched the two leave the building and he took out his phone. The phone rang twice, and the person picked up.

"What's up brother? Spike, you have a problem. A Detective by the name of Angel Spears, Criminal Division."

"Say no more brother, send me her info."

Nitti pulled on to a side street next to a high parking garage. The hospital was only a block away. He got out of the car and took a black case out of his truck. He looked around to make sure nobody saw him then closed the trunk. Spike's words echoed in his head like a CD on repeat. Nitti respected Spike but he honored Anton, but now his obedience to Spike's leadership had forced him to choose a side and he didn't like it one bit. He walked into the parking garage and headed up the stairway. He didn't plan to use the top floor, but he needed a floor that had little to no traffic and high enough to see the hospital's entrance. Nitti reached the fourth floor and peeked through the door. It was the perfect spot having only five cars and not a soul in sight. He walked over to the railing and peered across to the hospital. It would be a good spot to carry out his mission. He set the black case on the ground and put in the number combination. He glanced around the parking lot once more to make sure nobody was around. He took out the sniper rifle out of the case and twisted on the silencer. He lay on his stomach in between two cars and positioned his rifle. He was sure nobody could see him. He peeked through the scope. His vision was good. He glanced at his watch. The time was 11:45a.m. Anton and his men would arrive any minute. Nitti understood there would be no turning back. Once he discharged his rifle. The first bullet would undoubtedly seal his fate. A subordinate killing his boss was a taboo that no soldier could come back from, even if the order was given by the underboss. Nitti thought about turning himself in. He had done nothing wrong. It was Spike who killed Frank. The only thing he did wrong was dispose of the evidence in secret, but then he thought about how close Frank and Anthon were. There was no way he would let him live. He looked through his scope. A group of doctors and a few nurses were in front of the hospital taking a smoke break. They were having conversations and laughing with one another. Suddenly, he spotted what he was looking for. Three black Hummer trucks coming down the street and pulling into the hospital parking lot. He figured Anthon was in the first hummer. He definitely was not in the middle one because that would be predictable, and Anthon was never predictable. He watched the trucks park one by one. Four men got out of the middle truck and walked to the first one. Nitti smiled. He was right. He took a deep breath and looked back through the scope. Anthon stepped out of the truck and his security circled him. Nitti focused on getting Anthon in his sight when suddenly his phone rang. The Bluetooth played in his ear, but he let it go to voicemail. He watched as Anthon finally walked into the site and then the phone rang again. He took another deep breath and placed his finger on the trigger then the phone rang again.

"Hello." he yelled into the Bluetooth car piece.

"Were good brother!" A voice said, "About the mission." Spike ordered in a pleased tone.

"Are you sure?" Nitti asked. Anthon locked in his scope; all he needed to do was pull the trigger.

"Yeah brother, I'm sure. Darla is dead."

Nitti removed his finger from the trigger. Then he put it back. He pulled the trigger. The silver bullet whistled through the air. Anthon heard it but couldn't stop it. It split Anthon's head on contact and his body fell dead on the spot. His security pulled their guns and dragged his body between some cars. He peeked around trying to find the direction of the shooter, but by that time, Nitti already reached his car. He placed the case back in his trunk and got in the car and drove off. He drove the speed limit being sure to head in the opposite direction. He didn't know how Spike was going to take it, but in his mind, it was survival of the fittest. It was their lives that were hanging in the balance. He couldn't live a comfortable life knowing that one day Anthon could find out and their lives would be over. Spike better get ready for his promotion. He told himself. He deserves it anyway.

♀♀

THE DRAGON'S LIAR

Chapter Twenty

The flight to Nithael's lair in the Amazon only took him two hours. A distance that would have taken the fastest vampire five hours to travel. He transformed back into his human form and looked around the jungle. It was pitch black. Too dark for any creature using their eyes to see, but Nithael moved through the darkness with ease. Unlike the other vampires, he could see at night. He had a special night vision. He spotted the entrance to his lair. It was black with small rocks, boulders, and dirt. He burst through the rocks with his fist. The huge boulders turned into pebbles under his fists. He could have easily used the spell to remove the rocks, but he loved the feeling he got from breaking things. The lair was solid rock and marble like. A cold moist breeze blew through the dark cave with its many tunnels that led to places that only Nithael knew. It was the perfect place for a Dragon to lurk as well as many other wild animals. One of the tunnels led to a cave full of gold, relics, and other shiny stuff that Dragons like. The lexicube on the other hand lay on a black marble altar. The same place he left it two thousand years ago. The essence of his being craved the books power. The desire was unbearable. The worst part of his imprisonment was being away from the book. Its dark power was addictive and the withdrawal was agonizing. The first was nothing compared to it. He spoke a fire spell. (Tee-doke-na-raw) and a bright ball of fire appeared in front of him. It floated in mid-air. Its flame was a fury. Nithael took his index finger and rubbed it against his thumb and the flames became calm. With his middle finger, he directed the ball of fire over his shoulder. The fiery spear hovered only a few feet behind him. It followed him to the altar. He picked up the book, and its dark energy surged throughout his body, mending with the Lucifer DNA inside him which in turn made him stronger. He was already a force to be reckoned with but with the dark power of the lexicube he was damn near unstoppable. He sat cross legged on the floor his naked body immune to the cold. He opened the book to study it. The next time he encountered Zazriel, he would be ready.

♀♀

ANGEL GETS BAD INFORMATION

Angel and Domon got into the car. Suddenly Angel's phone rang. She glanced at the number and answered.

"Lenwood? What's up?"

"A tip just came in from one of my reliable confidential informants. They claim the man you are looking for, the Sterlin Park murderer, has been laying low in that abandoned Amazon factory by the expressway next to the toll road. My C.I. heard it from a third party, so I don't know if it's going to be any help, but I feel it's worth looking into."

"Thank you Lenwood!" Angel hung up her phone and looked at Domon.

"Good news!" she said. "Our killer may be hiding in an abandoned factory not far from here. I say we go give it a look."
Domon nodded his head then strapped on his seatbelt.

"Let's go."

He looked out his window and smiled. He knew there was no longer a Sterlin Park killer. It was Carlos they had killed in the park that night, which meant his plan was working. Angel parked about a block away from the abandoned building. They didn't want the killer to see them coming. They cut through a yard and across an alley. The factory was about two feet away. It was a square shaped building surrounded by a fence. It had a small parking lot in the front. They knew they could easily be spotted if they went to the front, so they followed the fence around to the back. Angel's first thought was to climb the fence but then she noticed a big hole in the fence.

"This way." she said.
Then she climbed through. Domon followed her through the hole and they headed to the closest door as they expected the door was broken.

"Somebody pried this door open." Domon said.

He reached into his shoulder holster and grabbed his 9. Angel took out her 40 caliber and readied herself. She looked at Domon and gave him a nod, a signal to open the door. Domon opened the door and Angel peered in. The coast was clear, so she went through and Domon followed right behind her. The Amazon building was big with a lot of doors going in both directions.

"I'll take left and you take right then will meet back here in the middle." Angel whispered to Domon, but he quickly refused.

"It's safer to stay together." he said.

“You take point and I’ll watch the hall and your back while you search the rooms.” Angel found Domon’s reaction strange. It would have been faster to do it her way. Once again, she got the feeling he knew something he wasn’t sharing with her. They didn’t have time for debate or to argue about it. So, she went along with it.

“Follow me.” she said.

They had just cleared the left side when he heard the sounds of motorcycles pulling up. Angel ran into one of the rooms and peaked through the crack of a boarded window. She could see the parking lot. Four bikers had pulled in and they got off their bikes and were headed into the building. The four men were armed with automatic weapons and Angel had a feeling the men were there for them.

“Get ready for an ambush.” Angel said. “Back into the hallway.” she aimed her gun toward the front door. “Four men armed with machine guns are coming into the building.” she said. “They will be coming through in a minute.”

“Instead of having a standoff, let’s take cover and catch them by surprise.” Domon suggested.

So, they headed to a room at the end of the hall. The room was big with lots of dusty machines. They took cover behind one of the machines. Their guns pointed at the door. They waited seeing that was the only way in and out. They had the advantage. The gunman entered the building. They whispered to each other as they searched room to room.

"She ain't in here!" one of the men said loudly. Another biker slapped him on the back of the head.

"Whisper you dumb motherfucker! She might hear you."

This let Angel know they were looking for her.

"They don't know I'm with you." Domon said. "Let's use that to our advantage. You draw them in close and I'll catch them off guard."

Before Angel could answer, he darted off and disappeared behind some machine. The Bikers walked through the door. They stood there looking around.

"This is Detective Spears!" Angel yelled. "I'm with the Sterlin Police Department. Slowly place your guns on the ground and place your hands above your head!" Angel demanded.

Her gun pointed at one of the men's head. She could get off one shot, but she'll have little to no chance against three automatic weapons. The bikers laughed and pointed their Uzis in Angel's direction.

"That's not going to happen Detective." one of them said, "And you won't be leaving here alive."

A flash went off, followed by a loud bang. Someone had thrown a flash grenade. Angel looked toward the gunman, but she couldn't see them clearly through the gray smoke, but they appeared to be coughing. She heard two shots then two thuds. Two of the bikers hit the ground. The other two bikers retreated to the hallway.

"Don't let them get away!" Angel yelled.

She pursued them down the hallway and Domon followed. The bikers raced to the middle of the hall. Then through the door that led them into the garage. Unfortunately for them, the garage door was shut.

"There is nowhere for you to go!" Angel shouted. "Drop your weapons and place your hands above your head!"

The men slowly put their guns on the floor and placed their hands above their head. Then Domon heard a buzzing sound, and then he caught a scent, a strong scent. Wolves hair, and a lot of it. The garage door began to open.

"It's a trap!" Domon yelled.

He grabbed Angel by her hand and headed back to the package room. Four big wolves stuck their heads under the garage door and wiggled themselves under it. Domon didn't look back because he already knew the creatures would be close on their heels. They entered the room and Domon slammed the door behind them, but it did little to no help. The wolves knocked the door down with once pounce. The wolves attempted to enter the room, but their paws were burned by the silver flakes that were on the floor. They backed out of the room and clawed from the door.

Domon looked at Angel and said, "We don't have much time before they figure out how to get past the silver flakes, so listen carefully. Your bullets are useless. If you must use them only aim for the head. The bullet won't kill them, but it could knock them unconscious. Here, take my spare." Domon handed her a Heckler and Koch .45. "It's filled with silver bullets. You got twelve shots. Aim for the head or heart, either will kill them, but be careful not to miss. We don't know how many we will encounter on our way out."

"What the fuck is going on?" Angel snapped! "There is a very big chance were not going to make it out of here alive. Those things are fucking vicious and huge!"

"Just trust me Angel, I promise I'll get us out of this." Domon said watching the wolves.

The wolves tried to get past the silver flakes for fifteen minutes, and then they finally seemed to get bored. Three of the wolves left, leaving only one that headed down the hallway patrolling the door. It paced back and forth not taking his eyes off Domon and Angel. Domon shot the creature in the eye and it died on the spot. Domon looked at Angel.

"It's now or never." The two headed down the hallway. The hall was clear.

"He could be in any room." Angel informed.

"Yeah, I know. Just remember what I said. Shoot for the head or the heart."

The two quickly passed by room from room. Their guns ready in their hands, but for some reason, the wolves weren't there. They went out the back door and headed for the gate but were stopped by two gunmen. They stood on the other side of the fence. Domon looked around and they were surrounded by armed gunmen whose guns were pointed at them. The men closed in and tightened their circle. Domon knew he could survive the shots, but worried about Angel. There was no way she would survive.

"Spread out!"

Spike demanded his men. Spike walked up to the circle.

"I see the Council sent their best killer. I'm flattered. I would say it's good to see you Domon, but we both know that's not true, seeing we are fighting on opposite sides this time. Before we gun you two down, I want you to know I won't take pleasure in giving you this warrior's death, but you know life's a bitch brother. So, don't take it personal, and on your way down, tell the devil I said hello."
Suddenly, Domon heard a voice in his head.

"Say tee-doke-ha-raw-ha."

Domon said it and everyone surrounding them burst into flames. They screamed in agonizing pain as their bodies burned to ashes. Angel stood there in shock.

"What just happened?"

"What do you mean?" Domon asked.

"You speak people on fire now?" Angel nagged!

"Out of all the shit you just seen from your attempted assassination too the werewolves, you're tripping over some people spontaneously combusting?"

"Yet you're the reason it happened! Screw your clearance Domon, you have some explaining to do! I want the uncut truth!"

“I guess I owe you that.” Domon said.

“You may not be able to handle the truth.”

“I find that hard to believe.” Angel said. “I can handle anything you throw at me.”

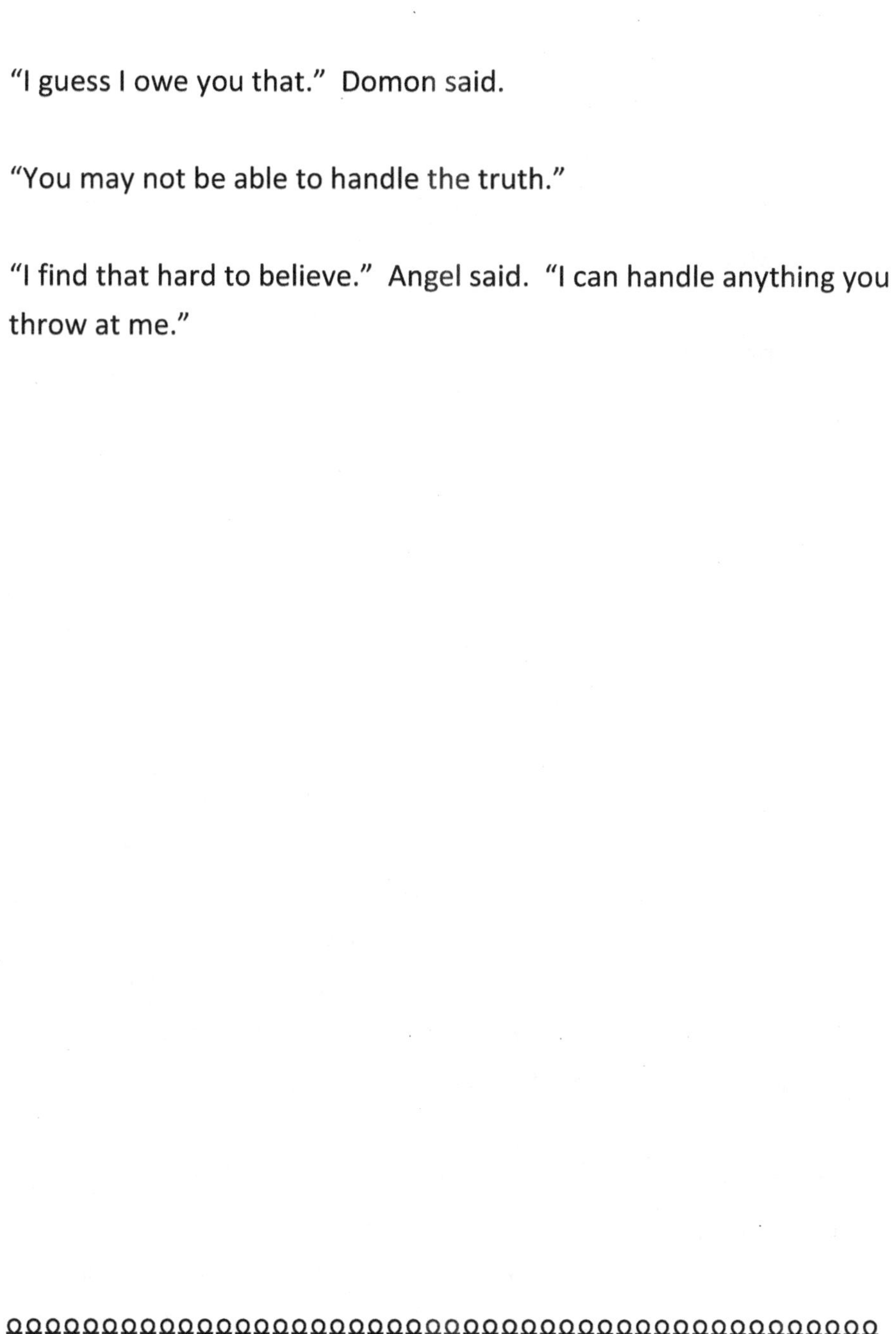

♀♀♀

EXQUISITE GOODS

Justin walked into "Exquisite Goods" and saw the owner dusting off some shelves.

"How can I help you?" The owner asked.

"I'm Justin Ray. The one Cardinal Peter called you about."

"Oh yes." he said. "You would have a letter for me."

Justin handed him the letter and he opened the red envelope and read it.

"Charles, I fear a great evil is coming our way. One the church is not ready for. I know that we are sworn by the church to keep its secrets, but this mans' prophetic vision has convinced me that Nithael the Blood Moon Dragon is about to return and we need to be ready. He was told in his dream to find the priesthood of Yahoel as if they still existed. Please help this man the best that you can. The fate of human-kind may depend on it, Sincerely Cardinal Peter."

Justin stood there for a moment as the owner read the letter, and he watched as he put the letter back in the envelope. He folded the envelope and placed it into his pocket. He walked to the front door and flipped over the sign that said open to the opposite side where it said closed and locked the door.

"This will take some time." he said.

They walked into the back room and Justin glanced around. The room was filled with old books and antique artifacts.

"Follow me." the owner said.

They headed to the next room which was the kitchen. There was a small wooden table and metal foldout chairs by the back door near the corner. The two unfolded the metal chairs and sat at the table. That is when the owner introduced himself.

"How rude of me. I'm Father Charles, but you can call me Charlie." "The Cardinal sounded worried in his letter. Therefore, I won't hold anything back. The Blood Moon Dragon's name is Nithael. We don't have his last name. Nithael is the first vampire and the father of all vampires and stronger than all the vampire races after him and is more powerful than the ancients, the originals, elders, even the Draculas'. It is said he is half demon and the first warlock and the only known apprentice and blood descendant to Lucifer. He sired many children and they spread across the world. Some becoming Kings and others claiming to be Gods, they ruled kingdoms and fathered savage religions. Their rulership began to dominate the world and with it, spread the darkness, along with creatures of the dark. The church knew it was only a matter of time before the human race was the minority and the world plunged into darkness. At that time, it was said that Lucifer himself would sometimes walk the earth along with the Dragon. The church looked for the Dragons weakness. Surely it had a weakness. All creatures of the darkness did, but they found none. Just when it seemed, all hope was lost for mankind, a prophet of Yahoel showed up to the Vatican. He said he was sent by God to deal with the Dragon. He asked for twenty of our best hunters and an army of Knight Templars. The Dragon was staying in his dynasty in Egypt when the prophet and his army waged war against the Dragon and his army. It took three days to reach the Dragon and once they did the prophet prayed down the Angel Zazriel, whose name means, Strength of God, from heaven. The Angel defeated the Dragon, but its essence could not be killed. So, the prophet bound him by magic and imprisoned him in a sarcophagus. His body was then entrusted to the Templars to be hidden so no one would ever find it."

"Do you think someone found it?"

"Yes, but that is the least of our problems Mr. Ray. The prophet is no longer with us. He passed centuries ago."

"Can't we just find a modern-day prophet? There are a lot of them around."

"No Mr. Ray. The prophets of today are much different than the prophets of old. Those prophets were born prophets not made prophets. Needless to say, the church has kept a relationship with the secret sect of Yahoel just in case the Dragon returned. Before the Angel Zazriel ascended back to heaven, he left his divine sword with the priesthood of Yahoel. They still have it to this day, but it can only be wielded by a Nephilim."

"You mean Nephilim as in half human and part Angel?"

"Yes, like it speaks of in the Bible."

"Where and how do we find one of them?" Justin asked.

"I don't know but I am sure we will figure it out. Have faith Mr. Ray. I am sure God will provide." the owner said. Suddenly, the bell on the front door rang and the two men looked at each other. They were sure the owner had locked the front door.

"Wait here." the owner said. "I got to check the door."

He walked to the front of the shop and a man dressed in Egyptian clothing stood in his shop. Somehow, he got in through the door.

"I've come for the compass." he said.

"What compass?" The owner asked now wondering if the man was crazy.

"The compass that will lead me to Lucifer's prison." the man replied.

Suddenly it made sense. He was standing in the presence of the Dragon. The Pharoah's outfit should have been a dead giveaway. Unfortunately for him, he didn't catch it. Realizing he had no way to escape, he tried to warn Justin.

"It's the Dragon!" he yelled.

The Dragon pounced on top of him and sunk its teeth into his neck. It needed him alive in order to see his memories which were stored in his blood. It got the information it needed then stood up and looked at the owner. The man lay on the floor, barely alive and without giving it a second thought and with one stomp, He crushed the owners face in. He walked into the back room. The scent of fear still lingered in the air, but the person was gone. The back door was open, and the persons scent trailed outward, but the Dragon didn't bother to follow. Instead, he pushed over the couch and found the loose board in the floor with his nails. He plucked the board out and took out the blue folded cloth inside the hole. He unfolded the cloth and there laid the compass shiny and looking brand-new. The needle of the relic pointed to the east.

"Looks like I'm going East." he said.

♀♀

JUSTIN HEADS TO JERUSALEM

Chapter Twenty One

Justin wasted no time leaving Sterling City. He got on the first plane to Jerusalem. Part of him was happy to have a recent get away from the Dragon but another part was concerned now that it was confirmed the threat to humanity was real. The death of Cardinal Charles and the theft of the compass forced the Cardinals to come clean and take his vision serious. The church set up a meeting for Justin to meet the secret priest of Yahoel. He exited the plane and the desert sun gave him a warm welcome and as Cardinal Peter promised, a monk from the temple of Yahweh awaited him. It wasn't hard for Justin to spot the monk because he was the only one in a hooded robe holding a sign. The small man held the cardboard over his head as if no one would see it while everybody else held their sign at chest level. Justin chuckled to himself and then went to meet the monk.

"I'm Justin Ray." he said. He shook the Monk's hand.

"Shalom Brother. I'm Yermiyahu. I'll be taking you to the temple. Do you have any luggage other than the bag you're holding?"
"No. Everything I need is in this bag." Justin said.

He shook the small leather suitcase. He was holding.
It was light with just a couple of outfits, underclothes, shampoo, a toothbrush, and a cheap hairbrush. Justin packed light. He didn't waste any time. The monk looked at the suitcase, and then nodded.

"Follow me. Our ride is outside."

They walked out the airport and a rusty Chevy pickup truck pulled up. It was white with a bunch of rust spots. The truck looked so old Justin wondered if it would make it out of the parking lot. He threw his bag in the back of the cab, and then climbed in with them. The monk hopped in the back.

"Also, how was your flight?" The monk asked, politely.

"It wasn't bad at all. I was surprised how fast I got here."

"Have you been here before?"

"Yeah, twice when I was a kid. Yeah, my parents came here to visit the Holy land, but the flight seemed much longer back then. Probably because I was a kid with a thousand things I would have rather been doing."

"Were your parents religious?"

"Yes, very religious. They were devoted Catholics, but I found my path in Christianity." Justin said.

"We all have our paths." The monk said. "What is important is we follow them."

"I agree." Justin said.

The monastery was surrounded by a big concrete wall. The truck pulled up to the gate and security let them in. It was a whole society built inside. They had buildings, houses, crops, walls, and everything a person would need to have a community. The truck drove down a long dusty road and pulled up to a giant church that looked like a museum. Somehow Justin knew it was the monastery. Everybody got out and entered the building. The place was a wonder, filled with ancient relics in history not known to the world, laid in cases on display for their community.

"This place is wonderful." Justin said in disbelief. He couldn't believe his eyes.

"Yes, it is!" the monk said "But, you can never tell a soul." "We are the seat of God's grace which you will soon see."

The two walked into a temple where a priest was praying to a golden box that had two golden cherubs on the top of it. Justin recognized the box on sight.

"You guys have the Ark of the Covenant." he asked?

"Yes, Brother Ray, we do." The priest stood up and then came to meet Brother Ray.

"I'm brother Aaron." the monk said.

"I am pleased to meet you."

"As you know, the Dragon has returned. He seeks to bring hell on earth and free Lucifer from his prison. I was told by Yah to entrust you with the map to Lucifer's prison and give you the Angel's sword which is encased in the casing over there."

He pointed to the casing to the right of the Ark. Justin walked to the showcase and looked at the legendary sword. It was a strange looking silver with a gold winged handle. It had a purple diamond ruby in the hilt.

"My God! It's beautiful." Justin exclaimed.

“I know! It was forged in heaven.” the monk explained. “It is nothing like you will ever see on earth.” The monk said. He walked over and took it out of the casing.

“I will give you the map to the pit. I was told to give you both the sword and the key, so guard them with your life and trust that Yah will guide you. We will escort you back to the plane tonight. You’re needed in Sterlin City. Peace be unto you, brother Justin, and may Yah bless your path.” the monk said. Shortly after, Justin was on a plane back to Sterlin City.

☥☥☥

ANGEL SUSPECTS DOMON USED HER

Angel and Domon walked back to her car and got in.

"Call me paranoid, but it seems as if you walked me into that trap." Angel said, looking Domon straight in the eyes.

"I'm sorry Angel, but I had to do it in order to draw Anton's men out."

"So, my suspicion is true. You used me as bait and put my life in danger!" Domon didn't reply. He didn't know what to say, and for some reason he felt bad about doing it.

"Did you hear what I said?" Angel asked.

"Yeah!"

"Why won't you answer then?"

"What do you want me to say Angel? I did what I had to do in order to draw Anton's men out. Carlos and Spike are dead, so your Sterlin Park murders are over. What more do you want?" Domon asked.

His job with Angel was finally over, yet it bothered him that they had heard about Anthon's death over the radio which meant his mission was finally over. He wondered how he would explain the incineration of Spike, but he knew he would have to come up with something good to explain it. No one would believe that something told him the words and he said them, and the people caught on fire. Angel could tell something was bothering Domon, but she didn't know what, although she was still mad at him. They managed to get the job done.

"Domon you managed to help me with this case while keeping me in the dark, but seeing this may be our last day together, I'm asking you to put me in the loop." she said. "I've seen too much to remain blind." Domon struggled to give Angel a polite smile.

"I'm sorry Angel, but it's safer if you don't know."

"So, you are not going to keep your word?" Angel asked, putting Domon in the trick bag. He had already agreed to tell her the truth. He shrugged his shoulders.

"What is it you want to know Angel?"

"You can start by telling me about the Council Agents. What is it they truly do and what you have been doing here."

"Once I tell you this, there is no going back. Are you positive you want to know this Angel?"

"I wouldn't have asked if it wasn't."

"You have already witnessed creatures beyond what you considered your reality. These creatures have been around for a very long time.

However, all these creatures are bound by laws to uphold a way of living in order to preserve all living races and balance all beings of creation, those of light and those of darkness. The Council consists of three humans, two witches, two wolves, and two vampires. They make the Constitution for all the living beings and when one of those laws is violated, a Counsel Agent investigates it and deals with it according to the Council Constitution. They wanted to expose our kind to the human world. They broke the laws by killing innocent humans. That's why I was sent to clean it up and make sure the human world never knows about us creatures of darkness or light.

"What kind of creature are you?" Angel asked. "Seeing you are not human, what you did to them wolves at the factory was something else."

"To be honest, I am a special vampire. One my race would call a fluke of nature. I have no weaknesses to the sun nor holy water or the cross. I can eat human food if I choose to. I don't have the thirst for blood like the average vampire. I don't know why once every few centuries, a vampire like myself comes through. My kind, make the best hunters, although we are rare."

"So, you are real life vampire?" Angel asked?

"Yes Angel." "One who doesn't need blood as a life force to live. I was sent here to take out Anthon and his subordinates for breaking the law and I was supposed to do so without anyone knowing."

"So why are you telling me now?" Angel asked?
She already knew the answer. She had found a soft spot in Domon's heart and he had found one in hers although she didn't know it.

"You asked for the truth, so I gave it to you." Domon said. "Your Father knew the truth. He was a great agent of light." Domon said. "I hope you can follow in his footsteps."

"It's as if you know my father." Angel replied. "You never knew him. So, don't talk like you do." Angel said.

"I'm sorry Angel, you're right. I'm only speaking of what Dillion told me and you are special, and I want you to know I truly enjoyed our time together." Domon said. Angel pulled into the parking lot and they both got out. Domon didn't have a car so he called a cab, but before he left, he gave Angel his cell phone number. "If you need my help, don't hesitate to call." he said, right before he got into the cab. Angel walked into the station ready to call it a night. There was a man waiting by her desk.

"Can I help you?" She asked.

"I am Justin Ray. I'm here to help you with the Exquisite Goods murder."

Justin explained everything that had happened starting from his vision and ending with the murder of Cardinal Charles at the antique shop and Angel didn't find it hard to believe after all she had experienced throughout the weeks and in her mind, anything was possible. Plus, she ran a background check on Justin Ray. He turned out to be a well-respected professor with no juvenile or adult record, not even a parking ticket. The whole situation was once again above her clearance. She had no idea what to do if she encountered this Dragon, plus part of her liked working with Domon on the crazy but top-secret cases. Angel picked up the phone and called Domon. He had just got on the plane when his phone went off. Angel told him everything Justin had said and Domon thought to himself that it was too big of a threat to disregard, so he got off the plane and headed to the Cardinals shop where he and Angel agreed to meet. Seeing no calls were made to the station pertaining to the break-in or murder, Angel, Justin, and a handful of Officers to do forensics headed to the possible crime scene. According to Justin, three days had passed, and Angel expected a contaminated crime scene, so she brought her best forensic team. The group of Officers parked in front of Exquisite Goods. The front door was locked. This was puzzling to Justin. Angel peered through the glass of the front door but the tint on the window, made it hard to see inside so Justin took them all around back. Just as he thought, the door was wide open. Angel looked at the Officer standing behind Justin.
"Watch him!" she ordered. "Don't let him out of your sight."

"Yes maam." the Officer said.

Angel and the remaining Officer went inside. They headed to the front with guns out, but nothing could prepare them for what they were about to see. They found a body, but the victim's face was crushed to pieces. Angel called back to the Officer standing which Justin.

"Cuff him!" she said! "We got a body!"

♀♀♀

THE DRAGON AT THE MUSEUM

Chapter Twenty Two

The Dragon finally made it to Jerusalem. He was on his way to a small city when suddenly the compass stopped working. He tapped it a couple of times against his hand, but the compass stopped working. He cursed the relic, and then threw it down into the sand. Finally, sanity came upon him. He walked the distance over and picked it up out of the sand. Once again, the needle started to work. This time it was pointing in the direction of Sterlin City.

"Fuck me!"

He used a new curse word he learned from the Priests blood along with many others then he shot off into the air. Domon didn't bother to take a cab or an Uber. It was much faster to fly to the antique shop. He landed a block over, and then walked the rest of the way. He walked past one of the squad cars and felt a strange energy emulating from the trunk. It puzzled him, but he stuck to his objective. There were about twelve officers on the scene. They had already surrounded the store with yellow tape. A man sat cuffed in the back of a squad car. Domon concluded it was Mr. Ray, and then he entered the shop. The forensics team was looking at the body and collecting evidence and Angel had been looking around the shop. Angel was kneeling down next to the couch when Domon walked in. She looked up and seen Domon standing in the kitchen.

"About time you got here!" she said, placing a piece of the floorboard in an evidence bag.

"You sound like you missed me." Domon joked.

"Yeah right!" Angel said. She stuck her hand in the hole in the floor. "Something was hidden down there. We got to find out what it was."

"I bet your witness knows." Domon said to Angel.

"I bet he does." Angel replied. "After we found the body, I had him arrested and put in the squad car. I wanted him to walk us through everything step-by-step once you got here." Angel explained.

She ordered an Officer to go get her suspect. A couple of minutes later, Justin was escorted back in. Justin walked them through the evidence moment by moment then they both concluded he wasn't strong enough to be the killer. Angel took him out of the handcuffs and questioned him once more. Justin, Domon, and Angel discussed a plan while the forensic Officers did their thing. Suddenly, the Dragon appeared. He walked through the front door and whispered some words and all the officers burst into flames. They burned to ashes on the spot. The Dragon walked to the back room and seen Angel standing by Domon, and Justin was sitting in a chair next to them. Their eyes peered at the Dragon, but they couldn't move. They were stuck in place. He spoke out loud and hit them with a freeze spell.

"Zeen-nah-cout-tee!"

He walked about the place with ease but to Domon and the others it seemed like forever.

"Give me the map." the Dragon said to Domon without moving his lips.

Domon realized he was talking to him telepathically. He could hear his voice loud and clear. Domon recognized the voice. It was the voice that told him the fire spell when they were surrounded. He couldn't understand why the creature would help him. The Dragon walked up to Justin and reached into his pocket. Domon tried to stop him but he was still paralyzed by the Dragons spell. The Dragon looked over to Domon.

"See you around." he said.

He took the map out of Justin's pocket then he transformed into a red mist. Domon watched the mist float through the opening under the door and disappear. The spell had finally broken, and everybody was free to move. Angel looked around the room and piles of ashes laid across the wooden floor, the remains of her fellow Officers. Angel had no idea how to explain what had just happened, but she knew it had to be reported. She took her radio out of its holster and began to call it in. That's when Domon grabbed her hand.

"There is no way you can explain this." Domon said. "I'll call it in to my office. They handle things like this."

"Thank you." Angel sighed. She looked at Justin.

"The Dragon could have easily killed us." she said. "For some reason he let us live, but I'm sure we won't be that lucky a second time. Before we make another move, we need to find a weakness and a way to kill it."

"The only weapon I know that can harm it is the Angel's sword." Justin explained. "I had it with me in my bag, but your Officer took it. However, we need to find a Nephilim to use it."

"What is a Nephilim?" Angel asked.

"It's a crossbreed between a human and an Angel. I take it you're not very religious?"

"Sorry don't have much time." Angel replied as they walked out the squad cars to retrieve Justin's bag from one of the Officers cars. Once again, Domon felt the energy coming from the trunk of the car. Angel took the bag out of the trunk.

"Careful with that." Domon warned.

"I am sensing a strange energy from that."

Angel took the sword out of the bag. Energy vibrated under her fingers. The sword began to glow in a blue and white color. She tried to let go of it but couldn't. Suddenly the blade grew longer. It had a yellow and gold glow around it. Angel wanted to panic, but for some reason she felt calm. She swung the sword back-and-forth. It made a whistling noise with every swing. Domon and Justin just stood there in awe.

"Looks like we found our Nephilim." Domon said. "Now we need to find that Dragon."

"I know where he is headed." Justin said, looking at the two. "There is an old church not too far from here. It's a historical landmark and I seen it on the map. You can bet he is going there to get the key. Fortunately for us, the map didn't show where the key is hidden, only the location of where it could be found, which means he will have to look for it, but we can go straight to it."

“So, you know its hiding place?” Angel asked.

“Yes!” “The priest of Yahoel told me where to get it.”

“Then we best be on our way.” Domon said.

The Dragon stood on the museum steps. The massive building reminded him of the Roman Coliseum. He walked up to the front door and peered through the glass door. The place was dark with the exception of the dim lights which shined behind the Museum displays. He transformed into a red mist and snuck under the doors. In mist form, he went undetected by the cameras and the security guard who was watching them. The mist floated from room to room until finally it encountered a security guard who was doing his rounds. He stared at the mist in confusion not knowing what to think. He watched the mist stretch itself finally taking the shape of a human body. In a panic, the guard reached for his radio and attempted to call it in, but before he could, a spirit like finger pierced threw his throat. The Dragon stood over the lifeless body then looked at the compass. The needle would move no matter what direction he stood in. It was a sure sign that the key was there, and the compass would be no help with finding it. He glanced around the room. The key could be anywhere hidden within any artifact and the place was big with hundreds of displays and items. He needed another plan and suddenly it hit him. He could hear heartbeats in the building. Perhaps one of them, seen or knew something that could lead him to the key. He looked down at the now deceased security guard and came up with a plan. The museum was quiet, and the guard spotted them at the front door. Angel and Domon flashed their badges and Justin gave a polite smile. The guard walked to the door and opened it.

"How can I be of assistance, he asked?"

"We got a call about a potential burglary." Angel said.

"Do you mind if we look around, Angel said?" The guard thought for a minute, then stepped aside to let them in.

"No, that won't be a problem."

The three walked in and Justin led the way. They walked from room to room until Justin stopped at a huge silver cross relic. It laid on display in the glass casing. Justin looked at the guard. The guard walked over to the casing. It took him three tries to pick the right key for that particular case. He had about thirty keys on his key ring so Justin couldn't blame him. The guard flipped open the door and stepped aside. Justin took the cross from its casing. It had three big rubies in the middle of it.

"Can I see your keys?" he asked Angel.

Angel handed him her car keys. Using the tip of a key, Justin plucked out the three rock size rubies. He placed the green one in the blue one's spot. The blue one and the yellow one's spot, and the yellow Ruby in the green one's spot. Suddenly the middle of the cross slid open, revealing a big silver key.

"This key was hidden in the cross centuries ago." Justin explained. He took the key out of the cross and looked at it.

"There are some words written in Hebrew engraved on it." Justin said.

"I can't translate all the words though."

"It's not much to see." Angel said.

"It looks like an old dungeon key."

Just put it in your pocket and let's go."

"May I see it, the guard asked?"

"He reached out his hand and Justin handed him the key."

"I'm a sucker for relics." the guard said with a smile.

He observed the key, and then closed the key tightly in his fist. At that moment, Justin realized he made a mistake. The guard pushed Justin across the room, and he slammed into a caveman's display.

Without giving it another thought, Domon lounged a series of punches at the guard, but he easily blocked them all.

"What the fuck!"

Domon questioned himself. No human could be that fast. The guard was now the Dragon. He was still wearing his Egyptian clothing. He gave Domon a quick jab to the chest and knocked him off his feet. Domon fell on his ass, but quickly jumped to his feet. The Dragon smiled then stood in a fighting stance. His attention was fully on Domon. He was so busy sizing him; he didn't hear Angel unsheathe the Angel Sword. Angel swung at the Dragon. The blade cut off his right hand. He jumped back.

"Zazriel's sword!" he yelled. "Impossible!"

He looked at Angel. She wasn't just a human like he had previously thought. Waves of blue spiritual energy flowed throughout her body. He recognized the energy.

"A decendant of Zazriel." he hissed.

He looked at Domon. They both were positioning themselves to attack him. Angel had moved behind him and almost in front of him. The two circled around him. With both hands he could easily take them both on, but with one hand and the Angel sword, they had the advantage.

“Zack-krown-de-pel!” he yelled.

Thunder bolts shot from the sky. It pierced the ceiling and scattered through the rooms, striking a number of showpieces. Domon and Angel jumped under some exhibits to take cover. The electricity bounced around the room, knocking out the lights. The Dragon took the key out of his dead hand, and then dropped it back on the floor, then disappeared into the darkness.

“I can’t see anything.” Angel complained, trying to see in the darkness.

The place was pitch black, but Domon could see in the dark. All vampires can see in the dark. He walked to the wall and flicked the light switch to the on position, but nothing happened.

“The lightning must’ve fried the fuse.” he said. “Stay here. I’ll get us some light.” he said.

Angel and Justin waited anxiously while Domon made his way through the Museum. Although the place was big, he searched the whole building within minutes. The generator was in the basement next to the fuse box. Domon cut the generator on and the place lit up. All the emergency lights cut on and Domon came walking into the room shortly after.

"On my way back, I found the security station." There were three dead guards and one of them looked exactly like the guard who attacked us."

"So, the Dragon can take on other people's forms?" Angel asked.

"It looks that way." Domon said, "But I believe he can only transform into people he fed on."

"Man! This guy keeps amazing me!"

"The more we learn about the Dragon, the better our chances of defeating him."

"I'm not going to just lie down and wait for this thing to destroy us." Angel said. "I say we go after him and fight till the end." Justin looked at Angel and dropped his head.

"I admire your determination." he said, "But the Dragon has everything he needs to destroy mankind. I'm afraid we have failed the human race."

"I wouldn't say that!"

A voice said walking into the room. A group of armed militant men dressed in military fatigues followed behind him. Their guns were aimed directly on Domon and the others.

“Lower your weapons.” the man demanded.

His troops obeyed the order. The general had a muscular build with a long gray beard. He looked like a character off the show “Viking”.

“I am General Grinds.” he said, “And we are Vatican Stealth Force. We were sent here to retrieve an object, but it looks like we got here too late.”

“Let me guess, you are here for the key.”

“That is correct Detective Spears.”

“How do you know my name?”

“We know everything about the three of you.” the general said.

“We have the best intelligence unit money could buy. Our mission was to get the key, but the Dragon was already here. Our orders were not to engage the Dragon only to observe it. So, we have been watching it. We spotted you two fighting the Dragon, but were ordered not to interfere, but when Detective Spears injured the Dragon. We were given the green light to help but the Dragon had already escaped.”

“So, you would have let him kill us?”

“Sorry Detective Spears but orders are orders and we are bound by God to follow them. Since you injured the Dragon, we have to take you in to speak with my superiors.”

“Mr. Justin Ray, your services are no longer needed, but if you have another vision, he handed Justin a card, you can reach us at this number. One of my soldiers is waiting up front. He will take you home.”

Justin looked at Angel and Domon. They gave him an acceptance nod. He did not want to leave them, but he was outgunned.

“What if I want to stay?” he asked.

“You don’t have the clearance.” the general said.

“Hopefully I’ll see you around.” he told Domon and Angel, then he headed to the front door.

The General looked at Domon and Angel, “Let’s get going.” he said. The three walked to the front and a soldier pulled up and the three hopped into the back.
“Take us to the prophet.” the general ordered the soldier in the driver seat. The soldier in the passenger seat stayed quiet.

“Why do you guys call him the prophet?” Angel asked.

"Because he is the last known prophet." the General answered.

"Yeah."

"He is rumored to be over two thousand years old."

The soldier sitting in the passenger seat interrupted, "Yet he looks no older than thirty-three." The general gave the soldier a stern stare. The soldier quickly turned around and stared ahead.

"Two thousand years old?" Angel chuckled. "This guy, I have to meet!"

☥☥

NITTI'S SAFEHOUSE

Chapter Twenty Three

Nitti sat out back of one of his five safe houses. None of the houses were in his name and no one knew about them except his realtor who also took care of all the paperwork. Nitti sat out on the wooden deck and just stared out at the water. He enjoyed the autumn weather. The lake was quiet and cool and soothing. Unfortunately, the fish weren't biting. He had been fishing for two hours and didn't get so much as a nibble. Nitti glanced around his lavish estate. It was one of his favorite places to unwind. The property was secluded and hidden deep into the forest with no neighbors for miles. The boat dock he used to fish on made the place so much sweeter. Spike wasn't happy about Anton's death. So, he ordered Nitti to leave town and lay low until things blew over. Nitti discarded his work phone on his way out of town. He stopped at a Walmart two towns over and bought a new phone. He had texted Spike and given him his new number along with the address he was staying at. Later that night, Spike called, and they discussed his new promotion to new under boss along with many other things, but that dream quickly crumbled when he heard the news of Spike's death from one of his loyal subordinates. Apparently, Spike and a group of his men were burned to death. Three days had passed since he killed

Anton and he wondered if it was cool to go home. Spike assured him that he was in the clear, but suddenly Spike was killed, and no one knew by whom. They said the Council Agent was responsible for the deaths, but nobody knew how. What if they found out and killed Spike? They could be waiting on him to return home. He definitely didn't want to walk into a trap, and he didn't want to miss Spike's funeral, even if his remains were only a handful of ashes. The barber suddenly moved. It dipped under the water.

"Finally, a bite." he said.

Then the doorbell rang. Nitti sat there for a moment. Nobody is supposed to know he's there. He walked to the door and peered through the peek hole. Three people stood in the doorway. The young native woman looked familiar. She stood at the door. No doubt, she was the one who rang the doorbell. There were two large Russian looking men who were clearly her security guards that stood behind her and that expensive limo was parked in the driveway. Nitti struggled to put a name with her face. He never forgot a beautiful face and this woman with the slanted eyes and the Pocahontas look. How could he forget? The woman knocked just one more time and then stepped back. The three of them stood there as if they could see him through the door. Then it dawned on him they could smell him. They were wolves.

"Nitti, I'm Olivia Parker, Anthon's sister. Open the door. I'm here to talk business."

♀♀

MEETING THE PROPHET

Chapter Twenty Four

The Jeep took to the highway outside of town, and then turned down an unmarked dirt trail. The trail led them to a monastery that was guarded like Fort Knox. A large fence surrounded the place and you had to pass a checkpoint of armed guards to get in. The soldier pulled up and flashed his ID and the guards let them through. The Jeep pulled up in front of the building and let the three go out. Angel stopped and looked at the building. It reminded her of an old castle. A monk came to the door and let them all in. The general escorted them through the building. It really did look like an old castle. He led them through a door guarded by two armed soldiers. He walked up to the two then nodded his head. The guards wasted no time opening up the two large doors.

"This is my stop." the general said. "I'll see you all later, when we do the briefing."

Angel and Domon shook his hand, and then the general went about his way. The two peered into the room. It looked like a study with bookshelves, couches and a desk. The room looked empty, but Domon could hear a heartbeat. He looked at Angel and they both walked in. A brown skinned man with short hair knelt on the floor praying. He wore a brown robe with a pair of silver prayer beads that he had tied around his waist like a belt. His head was looking towards the floor and he was mumbling something in a language they have never heard before. Suddenly he stopped, then listened. Domon and Angel were standing next to his couch and he was kneeling in front of it.

"That's why we didn't see him." Angel whispered.

"You caught me in the middle of prayer." the monk said, turning around to face Domon and Angel.

"Thank you for waiting." The monk stood up and walked over to Domon and Angel then shook their hand.

"I apologize about the manner you were brought here. I hope it wasn't too much of an inconvenience. Let's sit down." he suggested, sitting on one of the couches. Domon and Angel sat on the other, and then he got started.

"I am Yashiel, the last and remaining prophet of the priesthood of Yahoel. I've summoned you here because you two have battled the Dragon and not only survived, but managed to injure it, and now that you are both sitting here in front of me, I see why. Oh, how God works in mysterious ways." The prophet chuckled looking at Domon. "The sins of the father are definitely being punished by the son."

“Could you please speak plainly?” Domon asked, “With no riddles or metaphors that way we can get the full understanding?” Domon said, while Angel studied the prophet.

She looked at his skin. It was smooth and youthful and then at his beard and under his eyes. He didn’t even have bags. She looked at his hairline. It had not receded. There is no way this guy is over 30. Two thousand years old my ass, she thought to herself. The prophet looked at Angel as if he had heard her thoughts. He smiled, and then looked back at Domon.

“My apologies, Mr. Status. Force of habit. You both are radiating with spiritual energy. I felt you two when you were coming down the road. Angel, your aura is blue, white, bright yellow, and gold, which means you are an advocate of good and of angelic dissent. I once knew an angel with that same yellow and gold aura and he was a very good friend to me. I am guessing that is the reason you can wield his sword, which is a blessing for us because only a descendent of Zazriel can use this blade. The belief that any Nephilim can wield it is incorrect. Mr. Status, your aura is blue, brown, orange and red. The fact that you have no black means that there is still time to save your soul. Unfortunately, I’ve also seen that distinctive color of orange and red two thousand years ago when I faced your ancestor, the Dragon.” Domon looked at the monk like he was crazy.

“That creature is no kin of mine.” The monk gave him a smile.

"How many times have you encountered the Dragon?" The prophet asked.

"Twice." Domon answered. "Once at the antique shop and then again at the museum.

"And yet, after both incidents you managed to walk away with only a few cuts and bruises? It appears that Dragon even spared Miss. Spears on account of you. Perhaps he sensed a fondness for her in you? I believe he wants something from you Domon. I don't know what, but I fear it's something bad." Domon gave Yashiel a grimaced look.

"I don't have a fondness for Angel." he corrected the prophet, "and I don't care what he wants. I won't do it."

"Well that's good to know." the monk said, "But let me be clear, the two of you did not survive because of your skills. You're alive because he allowed it. The Dragon is perhaps one of the strongest beings on earth with extreme intelligence to match. He's able to transform, learn, and see memories from the blood of the people he fed upon. We need to catch him while he is still a stranger in our time. If he chooses to feed on the intelligence of the right people, he could become a bigger problem. I wasn't sure what he planned on doing now that he was free and awakened, but now his intentions are clear. He wants to free Lucifer and bring Armageddon upon the earth. If that happens, our world will never be the same again. It will be infected with demons, creatures of darkness, and worst of all, the deities of old. The good thing is he cannot find Lucifer's prison, not without Gabriel's horn. The prison is invisible to the naked eye. It will only reveal its location once the trumpet is blown. The trumpet has been hidden in a safe place, but we must catch the Dragon before it's too late."

"Why are we trying to catch the Dragon?" Angel asked. He is clearly a threat to all of humankind. Shouldn't we kill him?"

"You cannot kill the essence of evil Miss Spears. You can only kill its host, but if you do, I believe the evil energy will search for another body to possess. One whose DNA is compatible to its essence. That's why I imprisoned it while it was in the Dragon. I wasn't ready to chance my theory then and I'm still not willing to test it now. We must catch and bind the Dragon again. However, I will have our intelligence unit find a way to kill the force for good if that's possible." Angel looked at Domon. He seemed to be soaking everything up. He didn't seem very happy with Yahshiel's assessment of him.

"All of the options seem far-fetched." Angel said. "If we are not strong enough to kill him, how do you expect us to catch him? It seems our best strategy is to keep the horn hidden and safe."

"I wish it was that simple. Eventually he's going to realize he needs the horn, then he will come for us, and when he does, all it would take is one drop of our blood and he will know the horns location. One thing I know for sure, this is not going to just go away. He may have two- or three-days max. Just enough time for him to heal and figure things out, then he will come for the horn. I'm sure of that."

"Then we will be here to stop him." said Angel.

"You can't, Miss Spears, you're not strong enough. Even if you and Domon took him on together, you're still no match, not without being stronger and knowing your powers. He would kill you both in minutes."

"Then teach us what we need to know." Angel said willing to learn. "I already injured him once. I'm sure I can do it again."

"It's not that easy Miss Spears. It takes months, years, even centuries to grow stronger and learn the things you both need to know in order to defeat him and we only have a few days."

"So, what do you suggest we do because I definitely am not going to sit around and just wait for this Dragon to come and kill us." Angel snapped. Angel looked at Domon. She expected Him to back her. He nodded his head in agreement.

"I'm willing to do whatever it takes." Domon stated. "Just name it." Yashiel thought for a minute.

“Let me be clear. I’m not asking you guys to give up or do nothing because this problem won’t go away. I am only asking you give me until morning. I got a couple of things I need to figure out and to be honest I need you both well rested. I’ll have my guards escort you to our guest rooms. Feel free to roam the monastery. If you get lost just ask one of the guards and they will point you in the right direction. Be sure to rest up because we have a long day tomorrow and may God be with us.”

♀♀

SPENDING THE NIGHT

Chapter Twenty five

Domon and Angel followed a guard down a long hall into the east wing of the mansion. The guestrooms they would be staying in were close to one another and only a few feet away. The guard escorted Angel to her door first. She said good night to them both and went in. The room was humongous. It had its own bathroom with a walk-in shower and a big iron tub. Angel could tell that the room had been remodeled to fit the standard appliances of modern times. They didn't have a television, but they did have plugs. She plugged her charger in, then looked around. The linen on the bed was so clean and the place was spotless. Not one speck of dust anywhere. Angel concluded that the room was cleaned daily. Her phone battery was at thirty percent, so she connected it to the charger. She was about to log in to her Netflix account when she got a knock at her door.

"Who is it?" She yelled.

"Domon! Can I come in?"

Angel walked over to the door and let him in. Domon stepped in. There weren't too many places to sit. The only choices were the bed or big wooden trunk. Domon walked over to the trunk and sat on it.

"So, what's up?" Angel asked as she shut the door behind him.

"Things have been happening so fast. I just wanted to hear your thoughts on them." Angel sat across from him on the bed.

"To be honest, this is all new to me. I have just been going with the flow. I feel the weight of the world has been dropped on our lap and we have no choice but to fix it. That's if we can fix it."

"I agree." Domon said. "No matter what happens here in the future, I want you to know I have appreciated our bond, and I really don't bond with people. It's just there is something about you that gets past my defenses and makes me feel so strongly about you. I want you to know that no matter what, I got your back always and forever as a token of our friendship. I want to give you this."

Domon walked over to the bed and showed her a black, blue, and green friendship bracelet. Angel put out her wrist and he tied it on.

"I've always believed true friendship is bonded by a bracelet because it reminds us of that friendship. I made this in my spare time. I hope you like it."

Angel gave Domon a funny look like, what are you doing? Then she gave him a sincere look.

“It’s beautiful.” Angel said, looking at it on her wrist. She tapped the bed and invited Domon to sit on it. He sat next to her.

“Thank you for the bracelet.” Angel said. She put her hand on top of Domon’s and the two cuffed each other’s hands. “This means a lot to me.” Domon looked into Angel’s eyes. They turned from gray to green.

“I’m not going to lie. I felt some type of way since the day me and you were in the park that night.”

Angel leaned over and kissed Domon and he kissed her back. The two didn’t fuck. They made passionate love until they both fell asleep. Neither had a care about tomorrow. The thought never came up. The Dragon flew over Sterlin City. He wasn’t in full Dragon form. Instead, he was in vampire form which was a mix between man and bat. His dark black fur blended into the night and he went undetected as he glided across the night sky. He landed on the roof of a tall brick building. He opened his hand and looked at the key. Finally, he had what he needed to free his friend. He looked at his wrist. The nub was painful and healing slowly. He regretted not taking his hand, although the sword of Zazriel made his wounds heal slowly it would have healed a lot faster if he had attached his hand. He needed to feed in order to speed up the process. He couldn’t afford to be injured too long. He had already fed on the knowledge of the sailors, so he felt up to date. He now knew what a cell phone and a computer were and the knowledge that a library could offer. He planned on going to one in his spare time. A lot had changed over the centuries.

"Give me all your fucking money!" a man said.

The Dragon walked to the edge of the roof and looked down. A young gang member was robbing a civilian in an alleyway. A red bandanna covered his face.

"Please don't kill me." the man yelled.

"Shut up bitch and give me the money." The Dragon dropped down off the roof. He hovered behind the masked assailant.

"What the fuck?"

The robber turned around and the Dragon plunged his scorpion tail through his chest. The tail shot out the criminals back. His blood sprayed all over the civilian. The man screamed, then took off down the alley.

The Dragon smiled, then said, "Zeen-nah-cout-tee."

The civilian froze in place then the Dragon fed on the robber. The civilian would be next.

NITTI MEETS OLIVIA

Chapter Twenty Six

Nitti had no idea what Olivia wanted. He was somewhat scared to open the door, but he felt forced to. He opened the door to let them in. One of her guards stepped in first. Olivia came in second. The other bodyguard came in third.

"I bet you're wondering how I know about this place?" Olivia said with a smile. "Spike told me about it before he was killed." "You may not know this but me and Spike we're close. He spoke highly of you."

"Both Anton and Spike were good men." Nitti said. They walked into his living room and sat down.

"Can I get you guys anything, perhaps a drink?" Nitti asked.

"No, that won't be necessary." Olivia said.

"This won't take long. As you know my brother was the face of our legal Corporation. Now that he is gone, I'm going to need someone I can trust and rely on to be the public face of our company. I will continue to run things from the shadows handling the paperwork and finances like I did when my brother was alive, and you can be the one speaking at the meetings and interviews. I also give you my blessing as the new leader of the movement. How does that sound?"

"Like a deal, I can't refuse." Nitti said, blown away by Olivia's offer.

"Indeed, it's a wonderful deal." Olivia agreed, "But it comes with some conditions." Olivia's demeanor quickly changed. Nitti could see the fury in her eyes. "The first, is you shut down the raves and give shit time to blow over. The second, which is really the most important, you find the bastard who killed my brother and make him pay. A life for a life, you understand me?"

"Yes ma'am. Loud and clear."

"Then our business is done here. Congratulations on your new promotion Nitti. I'm looking forward to doing business with you."
On that note, the three left.

♀♀

THE TRAINING BEGINS

Chapter Twenty Seven

Domon and Angel were awakened by a soldier who knocked at the door. The two got dressed then he escorted them to a garden built within the West Wing of the monastery. The prophet Yashiel was waiting there, along with his prodigy.

"Good Morning Miss Spears and Mr. Status. This is Brother Aaron. He is my sharpest and most gifted student. He will be aiding me in your guys training. I won't lie. This will be the hardest training you to have ever endured, so I hope you two are ready." The monk chanted a spell and a portal appeared. "Follow me." he said, before he walked through.

The three followed him. The portal took them to a drastic land. Dinosaurs and giant planets populated the land.

"Where are we?" Angel asked shaken by the giant creatures that went about only a few feet away.

Domon stood there with his jaw dropped. He couldn't believe what he was seeing.

"We're in the Mesozoic Era. The Jurassic and Trassic period. The Dragon in his true form is huge and very strong. We are here to build up your physical strength and teach you graph magic which is a magic created through histogram symbols and parchments. I will also teach you to tap into your spiritual spark which will allow you to use your spiritual energy as a weapon and even modify physical ones. After this, we will work on your spiritual strength, and magic. I don't have to remind you we are here with little time. So, I need you two to give me your all. Angel I'll be training you here. Brother Aaron. You take Domon into the spiritual plane to train. On his spiritual energy, he and the Dragon share the same spiritual fingerprint which means he can tap into the Dragon's power and if he is strong enough even give the final blow."

Aaron nodded, and then took a small black pouch out of his pocket. He grabbed two purple rubies out of the bag and put the bag back in his pocket. He chanted a spell with both rubies in his hand and he handed Domon one. They both disappeared. Beams of sunlight gleamed through the cracks of the boarded windows of the abandoned building. The rays shined in the Dragon's face. He awoke, then looked at the bodies of his two victims. They laid side-by-side on the dusty floor. The abandoned building was quiet. Even the rats evacuated the moment he walked in. The Dragon looked at the key closely. A spell was engraved around the frame of the key. He recognized the language and he knew many tongues. It was the same language he had seen on the map. The only alphabet he knew better than all the others. It was ancient Hebrew. The Dragon recited the spell from both objects and then a blue X appeared on the map. Lucifier's prison had been right under his nose in the desert area outside of Sterlin City. He looked at his wound. His hand was forming. He just needed his fingers and a thumb. There is no reason to remain indoors. He had a whole world to see. Just then he realized he hadn't taken any time out to explore. He looked at the robber and the civilian. He liked the robbers face and the civilian's threads, so he transformed into the robber's face and morphed his body into a replica of the civilian's clothes. He walked out of the building and embraced the sun. He was in the middle of the ghetto. Some gang members were hanging on the corner of the street.

"A homey, you straight?" One of the members yelled.

The Dragon kept on walking. The Dragon was fascinated by the New World. So much had changed since the pyramids of Egypt, and although he had magic, he was intrigued with technology. He kept one of the victim's phones in his pocket although he had no one to call. He had Hulu and Candy Crush. He used the phone to Uber a cab downtown. He met the driver on one of the corners where there were no gang members. He got in and kept his hand covered. The driver was very talkative, but the Dragon didn't say much. He only nodded and occasionally answered questions. He thought about killing the driver because he wouldn't shut up, but then he thought against it. That would make things more difficult and he didn't need the heat, especially when he didn't know his way around. The Uber pulled up to the library and he got out and he paid the driver with the money he took from the victims. He even gave the driver a big tip.

"God bless you." the driver said.

"Far from it." the Dragon said with a smile.

☥☥☥

DOMON AND AARON BEGIN TRAINING

Domon and Aaron were transported into the spiritual world for lost souls. The lost souls lingered around and demons of the worst kind, tortured, and captured them. The place looked like earth except Domon found it hard to move and in this reality, spirit creatures lived among one another.

"Where are we?" Domon asked. "And why is it hard for me to move and breathe?"

"We are on the spiritual plane." Aaron replied. "The dimension that exists beyond our own. Our physical eyes prevent us from seeing it. It's hard for you to move because your spiritual energy is weak. It will be easier for you to move on to become stronger." Domon and Aaron trained for three hours and Domon felt like he couldn't go on. His body felt stiff and hurt all over.

"How much longer, he asked?"

"The fate of the world is depending on you guys." Aaron replied. Suddenly, Angel and Yahshiel appeared. Angel looked tired but toned and stronger.

"How's he doing?" Yashiel asked Aaron.

“He’s surprisingly strong.”

“Good, because we are going to need him to be.” Angel walked over to Domon.

“Is it me or is this place hard to breathe in?”

“We are on the spiritual plane.” Domon explained. “Apparently, it’s part of our training.”

“I take it the mobility is part of the training also?”

“Yep!”

Angel dropped her head. The training was truly hard.

“We will be training here for the next thirteen hours.’ Yashiel said.

“That will be the equivalent of three years.”

“Domon you come with me. Your training here is finished.”
Angel looked at the prophet like he was crazy.

“Thirteen hours? This is far too hard.” she complained.

“This is the only way.” Yashiel explained. “We have no choice.”

♀♀♀

THE DRAGON ENJOYS HIMSELF

Chapter Twenty Eight

The library provided plenty of information for the Dragon. He enjoyed reading the writings of countless authors. Suspense novels, philosophy, and romance were all a part of his favorite books to read. He was now a fan of literature and having the gift of a photographic memory and speed reading made the experience so much better. He spent the entire day at the library reading until the workers kicked him out. A grumpy old lady with pearl beads around her neck was the culprit. He would have eaten her, but she had a cross necklace on. He walked out into the night air, enjoying every minute of his freedom. The millennium was his era. He could feel it in his soul. He looked up at the night sky. The sun had settled in and the night had begun. He took out the map and looked at it. The blue X was still there. He looked at his hand. Three fingers along with the other were there, although his hand was still healing. He was confident he would be all right. He headed to the X on the map. It didn't take long for him to get there. He landed dead on the X. He looked around at the nothing that surrounded him. Desert land was everywhere.

"What is this?" He shouted to himself.
Nothing was around but desert land. The Dragon drew a pentagram in the sand. He summoned the demon Beelzebub.

"How can I help you my Lord?" the demon asked.

"Where the fuck is Lucifier's prison? The compass, the map, and the key brought me to this empty desert." The demon snarled then humbled itself.

"I don't know my Lord. There must be something more to this." he said. "Something that we missed."

The Dragon thought for a moment. There was something he missed. He flew right past it.

"God wouldn't have gone through the trouble of hiding the artifacts if it wasn't. Some of the closest people to God are monks. He adores the humble."

The Dragon knew the monastery being so close by was no coincidence. It was by design. One of them monks knew something, and he planned to find out what.

"Put your army on standby, the whole Legion." the Dragon ordered "and also send me two hundred of your strongest demons. I want that monastery and everyone in it."

“May your will be done my Lord.”

♀♀♀

THE FIGHT BEGINS

Chapter Twenty Nine

Thirteen hours of training felt like ten years for Domon and Angel, although they were, sore, they definitely felt fit and stronger. Yashiel opened another portal for them to walk through. This time they arrived in Yahshiel's study.

"Ahhh, right at home!" Yashiel said.

Domon chuckled. It was now clear to him. The monk was crazy. He walked over and sat on the couch. He was the one who did the rigorous training.

"I enjoyed training with you guys." he said. Domon and Angel looked at each other, and then slumped on the couch beside him. Suddenly, a loud siren sounded off and gunshots followed.

"Were under attack!" Yashiel yelled. Running to the closet and taking out his staff.

"I'll help the others." he told Aaron.

“You guys head to the vault and protect the horn.”

The pupil nodded. Then the door burst open. It was General Grinds with the group of soldiers.

“We have to get you to a safe place.” the General said.

Yashiel knew what the creatures were. Low level demons and there were a lot of them. The Dragon was definitely there.

“Don’t worry about me.” the prophet said. “We need to get to the horn.”

Yashiel walked into the hall. He stood behind the shooting soldiers. He chanted some words then lifted his staff in the air. A ball of light appeared.

“Close your eyes.” He yelled as the ball got brighter. It disintegrated all the dark creatures and those who disobeyed his order and looked. “Now you can look.” Yashiel said. Everyone opened their eyes. The hallway was clear, and the wall and floor were scorched with burn marks from a fire.

“We don’t have much time.” Yashiel told Grinds. “We need to get to the basement and protect the horn.” A trumpet blared off. A look of horror came across Yashiel’s face.

“We’re too late!” he said.

Suddenly the ground began to shake and the building with it. Everyone struggled to keep their balance. One soldier bounced from wall to wall. Angel cringed at the sound the bones made the minute his body smacked against the wall. Suddenly, the earthquake stopped. A soldier ran to a window and peeked out.

“The demons are retreating.” he said.

Everyone sighed at the same time. General Grinds looked around. His soldiers had already started tending to the wounded, so he went to help them.

“That was a good move.” Domon said. “He swarmed in with more than enough demons to keep us busy while he stole the horn. Now that he used it, what’s our next move?”

“I don’t know.” the monk said. He looked over at General Grinds who was helping his soldiers get on their feet.

“I have no idea where Lucifer’s prison is. We will help you look for it, but I feel it’s all in God’s hands now.”

“Sir?” General Grinds, interrupted. “A call just came in over the radio. An obelisk shaped structure just appeared out of the sand not far from here, and armies of them tar looking creatures are swarming around it."

Yashiel smiled. "There's our answer, but we must hurry. I fear we may be too late."

Vatican Stealth Force came with all the firepower they could muster. The attack on the monastery had been brutal. The backup from the Vatican Stealth Force support base was desperately needed but would take some time. Half of his men were killed, and a large amount were injured. He was forced to call all able hands on deck. Vatican Stealth Force support base had set back up but that would take some time and time was what they did not have. He deployed his two tanks along with every other powerful vehicle he had at his disposal. They pulled up only a few feet from the heavily guarded tower and jumped out the Jeep. The place was surrounded with two-hundred low-level level demons. They stood on guard. They saw a strange looking demon with three heads, one a ram, a bull, and the other a man. He sat on a big black bear dressed in armor. They paced back and forth in front of the entrance.

"The tar looking demons won't be that hard to get past." Yashiel said, "But that full-blooded demon guarding the door? That's Balaam." He is a terrible and powerful king in hell. He won't be easy to beat. It's going to take a tremendous amount of spiritual energy to defeat him, so I can't use the spell I used in the hall. We have to go in guns a blazing." He handed Domon and Angel machine guns.

"Let us lead the way."

"Use your firepower and save your spiritual energy for the Dragon. You guys will need it."

General Grinds gave the order on his radio. They ambushed the creatures giving it all they got. The demons put up a good fight, but specialized bullets blessed by a prophet gave Grind's soldiers the advantage. Yashiel lead Domon and Angel through the crown of creatures with a protective barrel. They could shoot out the bubbles, but anyone that touched it from the outside turned to stone. Finally, they reached the demon Balaam.

"Well! Well! I didn't expect to see you here Yashiel. I thought you would be dead by now." Balaam said, his human head smiling. "No worries. It's going to be a pleasure killing you now."

He slung his chained battle axe at Yashiel. The prophet moved in the nick of time. The demon tapped the bear and it pivoted sideways leaving the entrance to the tower unblocked. A mistake the prophet had counted on.

"Now is the time." the prophet yelled, signaling both Domon and Angel.

Domon grabbed Angel's hand and the two ran through. The demon saw them out of the corner of his eyes and that there was nothing he could do. The two had entered the tower and ran to the stairs. A handful of demons were guarding the stairs, but Angel slashed through them with the Angel Sword.

"Not bad!" Domon said, as they crept down the stairs.

"Shhhhh!" Angel whispered with her finger in front of her mouth. "We don't want the Dragon to hear us."

"I didn't need too. I could feel my kinfolks presence from a mile away. Have you come to take your place as King of our new dynasty, or have you come to help her fight for the humans?" The Dragon asked.

His back was turned to Domon and Angel and he stood facing the gate to Lucifer's prison. He placed the key in the lock and then turned it. Domon heard the clicking in the lock and wasted no time to attack. He lunged at the Dragon, clawed and full fingered, but the Dragon dodged his attack. Domon let off a series of punches and the Dragon blocked them.

"You've gotten faster." the Dragon teased.

Just then, Angel cut him across the back. The Dragon spun around, and Angel was right there waiting. She swung the sword at him. This time she missed by an inch. The Dragon jumped back then looked at Angel. Her spiritual energy was off the charts. That was the only way she had gotten close to him without him noticing. The Dragon uttered a spell to freeze time, but Domon countered it with a barrier spell. Angel smacked the ground hard. Her back slid across the dirt. Domon summoned the chains of hell. The black chains shot out the ground and the cuffs locked around the Dragons wrists and feet. They pulled him toward the ground. The Dragon dropped to his knees, then smiled.

"Nice!" he said. "Where did you learn that one?"

Angel looked at the gate. It was halfway up, and a giant clawed hand was pushing it up from the inside. She ran to the key to turn it in the opposite direction, but the key barely budged, probably because of the giant hand that was interfering with the gate. She managed to turn the key halfway in the lock, but no further. Taking its foot, it stomped down on Angel. The Dragon transformed into his Dragon form. His wrists and ankles burst out of the cuffs and the chains subsided back into the ground. The Dragon smacked Domon with its tail. He slammed him into a nearby pillar. The building rocked. The Dragon spun out his tongue like a lasso. It wrapped around Angel's leg. Unbalanced, she fell to the ground. It pulled her across the dirt with the intention of overpowering her. Angel twisted and turned chopping at its tongue with her sword but kept missing. Finally, it hit her, and she began chopping at the part wrapped around her leg. With one attempt, she hit her mark and cut the Dragons tongue. It let out a loud cry than its tongue went back into his mouth. Now angry, it swung its razor-sharp wings at Angel. The Dragon swung them furiously from side to side cutting through pillars and all. Angel dropped, ducked, and rolled to every shot. Unfortunately, she rolled into a corner and found herself trapped. With no place to go, she struggled for the next move, but the Dragon wasted no time. It lifted its massive foot and began to stomp down. He wanted to splatter her. His foot didn't touch the ground. A protective barrier surrounded Angel. A color of orange and red moved around it. Knowing exactly whose power it was, he turned to face Domon and he let the machine guns go. Just as the prophet said, the blessed bullets pierced through the Dragon scales. Domon could smell the blood. The Dragon stepped back, taking a deep breath. It blew ice from its mouth. Domon spun out of the way. He ducked behind a pillar, but the ice caught his left arm. It went numb and he dropped his gun. His arm was completely frozen. The slightest move could shatter his arm. He chanted a heating spell, but he knew it would take some time for his arm to thaw out. The Dragon knew what he was doing. He didn't intend to kill him, only to get him out of the way.

"Angel, I need you to have this." he yelled.

"Worry about yourself!"

Angel said from behind a pillar. After seeing what the Dragon had done to Domon. Only a fool wouldn't have taken cover. The Dragon turned his attention back on Angel. Using her sword, she sent a giant shockwave of energy directly at the Dragon's face. He threw up a wing in hopes of blocking it. The wave cut through his wing with ease and left a cut on his forehead. The Dragon stumbled for a second. He knocked down a few more pillars in the building and the building was starting to shake. Not wanting to disturb the building structure any longer, he turned back into his human form.

"Last chance Kinfolk, or die!" He yelled.

Domon didn't bother to answer. His arm was now completely healed, and he was more than ready to end this. Yashiel and General Grinds came running down the stairs with a handful of soldiers.

"Remember Angel don't kill him." the monk yelled. "We need him alive."

"This is over." Domon said. "Give yourself up and perhaps we can work something out."

"You're wrong, Kinfolk." the Dragon laughed. "We've only begun."

He chanted the words and demons appeared out of thin air. Hundreds of them. The soldiers started their attack and the Dragon walked over to the lock and turned the key once more. Again, the gate began to rise, and Angel was the closest to it. She fought her way over to the door and Domon followed behind her. He watched her out the corner of his eye while he fought the demons. Angel was handling her own with her sword. She was slashing demons left and right. She was clearly a worthy warrior. He looked over at Yashiel with his staff. He was punishing demons and killing them by the second.

"Angel? He yelled, Use the angel prayer."

Angel chanted the prayer and a white light from the heavens entered her body. Suddenly, she began to glow, and huge white wings sprouted out of her back. Her long brown hair had turned white. White as snow, and her body was covered with some kind of blue spiritual armor. Angel wasted no time. She attacked the Dragon head-on. She came at him sword and shield. The Dragon looked at her spiritual energy. It was as strong as Zazriel's. He felt a sense of panic but that was quickly dismissed with the hunger for revenge. He reached under his sleeve and pulled out his sword. It too was an Angel sword. A gift given to him by Lucifer. Angel swung her sword and clashed with the Dragon's weapon. Sparks of light glistened from the two as they fought on the ground. Suddenly, they took it to the air, their bodies flinging above the others. Domon chanted a freeze spell in hopes of jamming the lock. The gate was nearly open, and he had done it in the nick of time. Lucifer was now banging his head against the gate.

"Nithael?" He called. "Help me!"

The Dragon heard the familiar voice. He fought harder to defeat Angel, but she was a force to be reckoned with.

"Kinfolk?" he called. "You're going to betray your blood? Set him free."

Domon hesitated. He could hear the pain in his ancestor's voice. For a moment, he felt guilty and the Dragon felt it. He looked down at Domon and smiled. Just for a moment and Angel disregarded the prophets warning and plunged her sword through his heart. The prophet dropped his head and the Dragon let out a loud cry. His body fell from the sky and slammed against a pillar. The demons quickly disappeared, and the building began to shake.

"It's time to go!" Grimes yelled. "The building is going to collapse." He ordered his soldiers to evacuate the building and they all headed up the stairs. Everyone headed up the stairs, and then Domon realized they left the key. He turned around and headed down the stairs, but Angel grabbed him by the wrist.

"Where are you going?" She asked.

"I'm going to get the key." Domon answered. "We can't leave it here for someone to find. That would be too dangerous."

Angel released his hand. She realized she had left her sword, so she followed Domon down the stairs. She stood at the bottom stair while

Domon rushed and got the key. The place was shaking and on the verge of collapsing in. Bricks fell from the ceiling. Domon took the key and headed back.

"Grab my sword!"

Angel yelled as Domon made his way back. He pulled the sword from the Dragon's body. Until then, he hadn't noticed how much they looked alike. He took a quick mental picture and put it away in his memory, then headed to the stairs. Using his vampire speed, he rushed towards the stairs. Neither of them had seen the dark energy that exited the Dragon's wound. It hovered over the body for just a moment, and then shot off in Domon's direction. Angel had seen it coming.

"Look out!" she yelled, but it was too late.

The black jellyfish looking creature entered Domon. His eyes turned bloodshot red and he launched the sword at Angel. She jumped out the way and it landed against the stairs. Angel picked up the weapon and headed up the stairs. She knew what was happening. If only she had listened to the prophet and captured him. Domon took out his sword and charged at Angel. The two fought on the stairs while the building was coming down.

"Snap out of it Domon!" She yelled.

But Domon didn't reply. Instead, he fought harder. It seemed like he was no longer in control. He was besting her in the sword battle. Angel's spiritual energy was too low to use her Angel prayer. She mustered as much spiritual energy as she could and sent a shock wave of energy at Domon. The lash hit Domon in the chest and cut him in half. The blow knocked him off the stairs and he landed on the ground. In a state of shock, Angel stared down on Domon's lifeless body. She stood there as if it was some kind of nightmare she was waiting to awake from.

"Angel?"

General Grinds yelled. His voice broke her out of the trance. She looked up the stairs. Grinds was standing in the doorway. The stairs began to collapse, and Angel ran as fast as she could to the top. The last stair fell from under her feet, so she leaped for the doorway. She barely made it. The two ran out of the prison and the tower collapsed. The ground began to open, and it swallowed the place whole. Yashiel and the others waited a few feet away. Yashiel was the first to spot them through his binoculars. When he didn't see Domon he already knew what had happened, so he didn't bother to ask.

"I'm sorry." he told Angel. "Domon was a good man!"

Angel nodded her head, yes. She struggled to keep from crying.

"Mankind and our office owe you a great debt." Yashiel said. "If you need anything just ask."

Angel looked at the prophet and forced herself to smile. Although she knew the prophet could do many things there was only one thing she wanted at the moment. The one thing Yashiel couldn't give her and that was to bring Domon back. Angel slept at the monastery that night. It was the least Yashiel could do seeing it was unwise for Angel to be alone in the state of mind she was in. Yashiel spoke to Angel briefly before she entered her room, but she brushed him off. A clear sign saying she didn't want to talk so he let it go. The next morning Angel returned to work. She walked into the station and was told to report to Captain Dillion's office at once. The Officer buzzed her through the door and she b-lined his office. The door was closed, so she knocked. Dillion opened the door with a serious look on his face. Angel thought back to all the Officers the Dragon had killed at the shop. Perhaps Domon's people didn't clean things up.

"You wanted to see me?" Angel asked. Her heart was rapidly beating in her chest.

"Please have a seat." Dillion said. Angel sat down. "The DNA results from your headless perk came in yesterday." Angel tensed.

"Let me guess, it's not a match." Dillion smiled, then slammed the folder containing the DNA test on his desk.

"It was 100% a match on all the Sterlin Park cases." "Congratulations! Miss Spears. I never doubted you for a second; however, I have some good news. We would like to promote you to an active lieutenant." Angel thought about it for a moment.

"I appreciate the faith in me, but I have to refuse. With my skill, I belong out on the streets, not behind a desk giving orders." Angel explained.

Dillion laughed to himself. He knew why Angel turned down the promotion. Once you've seen behind the curtain, it's hard to just sit around and live like you don't know. Dillion had also had a problem doing so once he became a Captain. He gave Angel a polite smile.

"I understand, and I'll let them know." "Is there anything else I can do for you?"

"Yes Captain." Angel dropped her head down. She fought to hold the tears back. The grief from everything was weighing down on her. She struggled to keep from breaking down. Wiping the tears from her eyes, "I would like to take my leave."

☥☥☥

Coming Soon!

Legend of the Sleeping Dragon Book 2

If you loved book one and could not get enough, check out the sequel for this and more books to come. You can order these and much more from New Nationwide Publishings No. 1. The author would love to interact with you and get your input on the book.

Visit our website at...
https://newnationwidepublishing1.com

Visit the Author's Facebook page...
https://www.facebook.com/lasalle.johnson.5621

Visit the Author on Twitter...
https://twitter.com/johnson_lasalle

www.ingramcontent.com/pod-product-compliance
Lightning Source LLC
LaVergne TN
LVHW091127080826
845145LV00008B/2071

* 9 7 8 1 7 3 5 3 9 2 0 1 1 *